A WORLD FULL OF SPOOKY STORIES

WRITTEN BY ANGELA McALLISTER
ILLUSTRATED BY MADALINA ANDRONIC

Frances Lincoln
Children's Books

CONTENTS

INTO THE WOODS

Hansel and Gretel (Germany) — 6
Grandfather's Eyes (Czech Republic) — 9
Vasilissa the Beautiful (Russia) — 11
The Treasure Thief (Egypt) — 16
Little Red Riding Hood (Germany) — 18

DOWN BY THE WATER

The Story of the Yara (Brazil) — 20
The Cold Lady (Japan) — 23
The Bunyip (Australia) — 25
The Snake Prince (India) — 28
Morag and the Water Horse (Scotland) — 31

ENCHANTED PLACES

Tam Lin (Scotland) — 34
The Dance of Death (Canada) — 36
The Lady of the Lake (Wales) — 38
The Water Witch (France) — 40
The Maiden in the Pagoda (China) — 44
The Talking Skull (West Africa) — 46

STRANGERS AT THE DOOR

The Enchanted Apple Tree (France) — 48
The Blacksmith and the Demon (Russia) — 50
The Girl and the Chenoo (Native American (Passamaquoddy)) — 52
The Horned Women (Ireland) — 55
The Blind Man and the Demons (Korea) — 58
The Clever Goldsmith (Syria) — 60

IN FARM AND FIELD

Yallery Brown (England) — 62
Old Nick and the Girl (Norway) — 64
The Elder Tree Witch (England) — 67
The Snake (India) — 71
The Bogey Beast (England) — 72

HOME OF THE SPIRITS

The Spirit of the Singing House (Canada (Inuit)) — 74
The Ghost Land (Alaska) — 75
Herne the Hunter (England) — 76
The Night on the Battlefield (China) — 80

GRAVEYARD

Teig O'Kane and the Corpse (Ireland)   82

The Grave Mound (Germany)   86

The Place Where There Were No Graves (Egypt)   87

The Ghost and the Moneybox (Iceland)   88

Counting out the Bodies (Bermuda)   90

UPON THE OCEAN, UNDER THE SEA

The Giantess and the Stone Boat (Iceland)   92

The Sea Goblins (New Zealand)   95

The Sea Nymph (Sweden)   97

The Spectre Ship (Germany)   98

The Seal Wife (Scotland)   102

FROZEN LANDS

The Red Skeleton (Alaska)   104

The Ice King (Canada (Mi'Kmaq))   105

The Guest (Canada)   108

IN CASTLE HALL

Esteban and the Ghost (Spain)   110

Sir Gawain and the Green Knight (England)   112

Rumpelstiltskin (Germany)   116

ON A MOUNTAIN PATH

The Old Ogre (China)   118

Amin and the Ghoul (Persia)   120

The Girl who Turned to Stone (Chile)   123

APPENDIX

Sources   126

FOR MY SISTER-IN-LAW PAULA, WHO WORKS WITH GREAT DEDICATION TO LITERACY

ABOUT THE AUTHOR

Angela McAllister is the author of over 80 books for children of all ages. Her books have been adapted for the stage, translated into more than 20 languages, and have won many awards.

ABOUT THE ILLUSTRATOR

Originally from Romania, Madalina Andronic currently lives in Italy. She draws inspiration from folklore, love and travelling. She is passionate about details and rich colours, and her art radiates with energy and love. With an MA in Illustration from Camberwell College of Arts, London, she has developed a strong and distinctive style and has worked for clients all around the world.

ACKNOWLEDGEMENTS

With thanks to Luke and Eleanor for sharing this spooky journey — A.M.

INTO · THE
WOODS

INTO THE WOODS

EUROPE

A STORY FROM GERMANY

HANSEL AND GRETEL

Hansel and Gretel lived with their father and stepmother beside a great forest.

One night their father, who was a poor woodcutter, told his wife that they had no money left. "I don't know how we shall feed ourselves," he sighed.

His wife had no love for Hansel and Gretel and saw this as a chance to be rid of them. "We must take the children into the forest tomorrow and leave them there," she told her husband. "Then we'll only have two mouths to feed."

The woodcutter tried to protest but his wife wouldn't listen. "If you refuse, husband, all four of us shall starve," she said.

Hansel and Gretel overheard their stepmother's plan.

"Don't worry, Hansel," said Gretel, "I'll look after you." She put on her jacket, crept out into the moonlit garden and filled her pockets with white pebbles.

Next morning, as the family walked into the forest, Gretel secretly dropped the pebbles along the path. When they were deep in the woods the stepmother told Hansel and Gretel to rest. "Wait here while your father and I cut some wood," she said.

Hansel and Gretel waited all day but no one came to fetch them. "We'll never find our way home alone," cried Hansel. However, when night fell and the moon appeared, Gretel's white pebbles glowed brightly, showing them the path home.

Hansel and Gretel arrived home tired and hungry, only to receive a scolding from their stepmother. "It's your own fault. We called but you didn't come," she snapped.

The following day, she insisted that they return to the forest. This time, Gretel didn't have a chance to gather any pebbles, so she took a crust of bread from the kitchen and dropped crumbs along the path.

Once more, the children were left in the forest. But when evening came and the moon appeared there wasn't one breadcrumb to be seen, for birds had eaten them all.

"I'm sure we shall find our own way home," said Gretel bravely.

Hansel and Gretel set off through the

INTO THE WOODS

forest. Before long, they smelled something sweet and delicious. To their surprise, they found a house made of golden gingerbread with a roof of little cakes. The children were so hungry that they broke off pieces to eat.

At once an old woman opened the door. She smiled kindly at them. "If you are hungry my dears, come inside," she said.

Hansel and Gretel stepped into the gingerbread house. The old woman gave them sugared pancakes and apple tart and then offered them two soft beds. Soon they were fast asleep.

Early next morning, however, the children discovered they'd been tricked by a witch! The old woman pulled Hansel out of bed and locked him in a stable. Then she ordered Gretel to cook for her. "When your brother is fattened up I shall eat him!" she declared.

There was no escape. Every day, Hansel had to stick his finger through a hole so the witch could feel how plump he'd grown, but he cleverly poked a bone from his dinner out instead. The witch had bad eyesight and was easily fooled but after four weeks she grew impatient.

"Today I shall eat that boy, fat or thin," the witch told Gretel. "Climb into the oven, girl, to see if it is hot."

Gretel suspected the witch intended to cook her first. "The oven door is stuck," she replied.

"Nonsense!" snapped the witch. She bent down and opened it. In an instant, Gretel pushed her into the hot oven and slammed the door shut.

Then Gretel released Hansel from the stable. Together they explored the gingerbread house and found jewels to fill their pockets.

Meanwhile, the woodcutter had been desperately worried about his children. When his wife suddenly fell ill and died, he came to search for them in the forest.

To his joy, he found Hansel and Gretel searching for the path home. Thanks to the witch's jewels, the woodcutter's family never went hungry again.

EUROPE
A STORY FROM CZECH REPUBLIC

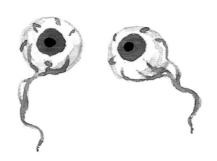

GRANDFATHER'S EYES

Yanachek was alone in the world. One day, he met an old Grandfather sitting outside a cottage who had empty holes where his eyes had been.

"Do you have any work for me?" asked Yanachek.

"I need someone to take my hungry goats to the meadow," said the blind man, so Yanachek agreed to tend to his goats.

The blind old man was grateful. "But don't go near the hill in the woods," he warned, "or the Yezinkas will catch you. Those wicked witches stole my eyes!"

"Don't worry about me," said Yanachek cheerfully, "I can look after myself."

At first, Yanachek grazed the goats in the meadow nearby but one morning he decided to find them better grass to eat on the hill. "I'm not afraid of any Yezinkas," he thought.

First, he cut three long bramble branches and wound them around the crown of his hat, then he drove the goats through the wood to the hill.

As Yanachek sat watching the goats graze, a beautiful maiden stepped out of the woods. "Here's an apple for you, shepherd boy," she said.

Yanachek guessed that she must be a Yezinka out to trick him.

"No thank you," he replied. "My master gives me all the apples I want."

Seeing that he couldn't be persuaded, the maiden vanished.

A short while later, another maiden appeared and offered him a red rose.

Yanachek refused it. "My master's garden is full of roses," he said. At these words the maiden vanished.

Then a third maiden appeared, carrying a golden comb. "Let me comb your hair, shepherd boy," she said.

Yanachek took off his hat. However, when the maiden came close, he quickly unwound a bramble branch and tied her hands with it, for he knew that a Yezinka

INTO THE WOODS

cannot move if she is struck by a bramble.

"Help, sisters!" cried the Yezinka. The other two maidens came running but Yanachek was ready with more bramble branches and quickly tied them up too. Then he ran home to fetch the old man.

Yanachek led the blind man through the wood to the hill where the Yezinkas were struggling in vain. "Tell me where my master's eyes are," said Yanachek.

The first maiden agreed to show him. She led them along the bank of a deep river to a cave where she and her sisters had collected an enormous pile of eyes. She picked out a pair for the old man.

However, when he looked through them the old man gasped in horror. "I see dark treetops, moths and bats," he cried. "These are not my eyes, they are owls' eyes! Take them out!"

So Yanachek took them out and threw the maiden into the river.

Then the second maiden chose a pair of eyes from the pile. When the old man looked through them he shook with terror.

"I see tangled bushes, snapping teeth and hot red tongues," he cried. "These are not my eyes, they are wolves' eyes! Take them out!"

So Yanachek took them out and threw the second maiden into the river.

Then the third maiden chose a pair of eyes. When the old man looked through them he trembled with fear.

"I see murky water, swirling weeds and flashing fins," he cried. "These are not my eyes, they are fishes' eyes! Take them out!"

But the third maiden didn't want to follow her sisters into the river. She begged Yanachek to try another pair.

This time, the old man looked and smiled. "At last I see the hill and my goats and my good friend Yanachek," he said. "These are my own dear eyes!"

So Yanachek released the Yezinka and then he and the old man returned home to live happily together.

EUROPE
A STORY
FROM RUSSIA

VASILISSA THE BEAUTIFUL

Vasilissa was the only child of a merchant and his wife. When she was eight years old, her mother became very ill. Vasilissa's mother took a little wooden doll from beneath her pillow and gave it to her daughter.

"Keep this doll a secret and look after it well," she told Vasilissa. "Soon I must leave you, but if you are ever in trouble and need advice, feed the little doll, tell it your worries and it will help you." Then she kissed her daughter and gave her a blessing. A few days later, Vasilissa's mother died.

Time passed. The merchant grew lonely so he married another wife, a widow who had two daughters of her own. "I hope she will be a good mother to you," he told Vasilissa.

But the merchant had chosen unwisely, for the widow was really a cold, cruel woman who had only married him for his wealth. She and her daughters became jealous of Vasilissa, who had grown into a beautiful girl, so they treated her harshly and gave her work to do outside in the sun and wind, hoping she would lose her beauty.

Vasilissa never complained but one night she remembered the little doll her mother had given her. She fed it some crumbs of bread. Suddenly, the little doll's eyes shone like fireflies. "My stepmother hates me," Vasilissa told the little doll, "what shall I do?"

"Forget your troubles and sleep," the little doll replied. "The morning is wiser than the evening." And from that day, the little doll secretly helped Vasilissa with her work.

After a few months, the merchant announced that he had to make a long journey to a distant land. As soon as he was gone, the stepmother sold his house and moved the family far away to the edge of a dark forest. Vasilissa was filled with despair but she fed the little doll and it listened to her troubles and comforted her.

At the heart of the forest, in a house that stood on a pair of chicken's legs, lived an old witch

INTO THE WOODS

called Baba Yaga. Nobody ever went near the house, afraid that they would be caught and eaten. However, Vasilissa's stepmother began sending her into the forest each day to collect a basket of nuts and berries, hoping that she would be caught by Baba Yaga and never seen again. Luckily, Vasilissa's little doll showed her how to fill her basket without straying close to the witch's house. But Vasilissa's safe return only made her stepmother hate her more.

Before long, the stepmother devised another plan to get rid of Vasilissa. One evening, she let the fire in the stove go out. "Now we don't have a flame to light a candle or cook the dinner," she complained. "Vasilissa must go into the forest to get a light from Baba Yaga." Vasilissa was terrified but her stepsisters refused to go and pushed her out of the door.

Alone in the dark, Vasilissa took the little doll from her pocket and fed it some berries. The little doll's eyes shone like glow-worms. "Don't be afraid, Vasilissa," it said. "Do as you have been told. No harm can come to you as long as I am with you."

Vasilissa set off bravely to find Baba Yaga's house. As night fell, the forest came alive with shadowy creatures. Clutching the little doll, Vasilissa walked on, deep into the woods.

After several hours, she suddenly saw a horseman in white robes gallop out of the trees on a white steed. As he passed, the first light of dawn appeared.

Vasilissa continued, further into the forest. A short while later, a second horseman, dressed in red, rode by on a red steed and as he passed, the sun rose in the sky.

Still Vasilissa walked on, searching for Baba Yaga. At last, as twilight fell, she came to a clearing in which stood a house on chicken's legs, surrounded by a fence of dead men's bones. Along the fence hung hollow-eyed skulls and the lock at the gate was a jaw filled with sharp teeth. Vasilissa froze in terror. Suddenly, a third horseman dressed in black rode up on a black steed. He passed through the gate and night descended. At once, the eyes of the skulls began to glow brightly and the trees rustled and moaned. Out of the forest flew the witch, Baba Yaga, sitting in a mortar which she steered along with a pestle. She swayed from side to side sweeping away her trail with a broom and when she reached the clearing she stopped and sniffed the air. "Who's hiding at my gate?" she cried.

Vasilissa stepped out of the shadows, trembling with fear. "My stepmother sent me to ask for a light," she said.

Baba Yaga stared hard at Vasilissa. "Ah yes, I know where you come from," she muttered, "but if you want a light you must work for me awhile, otherwise I shall eat you for my supper." With that, she commanded the gates to open and flew through. Vasilissa shuddered. Gripping the doll in her pocket, she followed the witch and heard the jaws of the gate lock behind her.

In the house, Baba Yaga told Vasilissa to prepare her supper. The witch ate enough meat for a dozen people, but there was only a little cabbage soup and a crust of bread for Vasilissa.

"While I am away tomorrow, you must clean the house, sweep the yard and pick all the wild peas out of my sack of wheat," she told Vasilissa. Then the bony old witch lay on top of the stove and shut her eyes.

When Vasilissa was sure that Baba Yaga was asleep, she took the little doll out of her pocket and fed it the last spoonful of soup. The little doll's eyes shone like candles. "I'm so afraid," said Vasilissa. "If I don't do everything Baba Yaga has asked, she'll eat me for her supper."

"Don't worry, sleep now," said the little doll. "The morning is wiser than the evening."

Next morning, Vasilissa woke before it was light. She saw the white horseman gallop across the clearing and leap the fence. As he disappeared into the forest, dawn appeared and the lights of the skulls' eyes dimmed.

At the gate, Baba Yaga climbed into her mortar and whistled for her pestle and broom. Then the red horseman galloped across the clearing and the sun rose. Vasilissa watched Baba Yaga fly away. With a heavy heart she wondered how to manage all the tasks she'd been given but, to her relief, she saw that the little doll had already done them all.

That evening, the black horseman galloped across the clearing and night fell. The skulls glowed and Baba Yaga returned. To her annoyance, she couldn't find anything to complain about. She called for her servants and three hands appeared to carry away the sack of wheat.

Next day, Baba Yaga gave Vasilissa more tasks. "When you've swept the house and the yard, take my sack of poppy seeds and clean the earth off every one," she told Vasilissa. "If they are not clean, I will eat you for supper."

Once more, the little doll did the work and that evening there was nothing for the witch to complain about. She called for her servants and the three hands carried away the sack of poppy seeds.

When Baba Yaga had eaten her supper she peered closely at Vasilissa, "Speak, child," she said, "I see you have a question, but remember, not every

question has a good answer."

"I wish to know who is the white horseman," said Vasilissa nervously.

"That is my servant, Bright Day," answered Baba Yaga. "He cannot hurt you."

"And who is the red horseman?" asked Vasilissa.

"That is my servant, Red Sun," answered Baba Yaga. "He cannot hurt you."

"Then who is the black horseman?" asked Vasilissa.

"That is my servant, Dark Night," answered Baba Yaga. "He cannot hurt you either. Ask me another question."

Vasilissa was curious to know about the three hands but she remembered that not every question has a good answer and remained silent.

Baba Yaga scowled. "It's lucky for you that you didn't ask about my other servants, the three hands, otherwise they would have taken you off to be my supper, just like the wheat and poppy seeds." Then the old witch asked Vasilissa how she was able to do all the tasks she'd been given so perfectly.

Vasilissa saw Baba Yaga staring at her pocket but stopped herself from giving her secret away. "The blessing of my mother helps me," she answered.

At these words, the old witch screamed as if she was in pain. "I'll have nobody with a blessing in this house," she shrieked. "Get out and be gone!"

Vasilissa ran out of the house and across the clearing. As she reached the gate, Baba Yaga commanded it to open and threw a skull with burning eyes after her. "There is the fire you came for," she cried. "Your stepmother may have the joy of it!"

Vasilissa put the shining skull on the end of a stick and hurried away home through the forest. She walked all through the night and the following day. At last, as evening fell she came to the edge of the forest and found her stepmother's house. Thinking that the stepmother must have found fire herself after all that time, Vasilissa threw the skull away among the bushes. But, to her surprise, it spoke to her.

"Don't throw me away, beautiful Vasilissa," said the skull. "Take me to your stepmother." So she picked it up and carried it into the house.

Vasilissa's stepmother and stepsisters were very pleased to see her. Since the night Vasilissa left, they had been unable to keep a fire alight in the house, no matter how they tried and they were very cold and hungry. The stepmother took the witch's fire and lit a candle.

To her relief, the candle stayed alight. But once the skull was in the house, its eyes started to burn like red-hot coals. It stared at the stepmother and her daughters. No matter which way they turned, the eyes began to burn into them, hotter and hotter, fierce as a furnace, until suddenly all three of them caught fire and were burnt to ashes.

Next morning, Vasilissa buried the ashes and the witch's skull. As she wiped the earth from her hands she heard a cry from the path. There stood her father, who had long been searching for his Vasilissa, overjoyed to be reunited with her at last.

The merchant promised never to leave his daughter again and she kept the little wooden doll in her pocket for the rest of her days.

ASIA & AFRICA
A STORY FROM EGYPT

THE TREASURE THIEF

In ancient Egypt there once lived a king called Rhampsinit, who was very wealthy. In order to keep his riches safe, he asked for a treasure house to be built.

The master builder set to work but he couldn't resist the temptation to steal a little gold and silver for himself, so he placed one of the building's stones in such a way that it could be removed from the outside, giving him a secret entrance.

However, soon after the treasure house was finished and the king's riches were put inside, the master builder fell ill. Knowing he was going to die, he told his two sons how to find the secret stone.

After their father died, the two sons went to the treasure house one night, removed the loose stone and climbed inside. They filled bags with all the silver and gold they could carry and then hurried home. The next night, the two thieves went back for more.

When Rhampsinit discovered that some of his treasure had been stolen he was furious. Nobody

could explain how it was taken from a locked, guarded building and so the king ordered traps to be hidden inside to catch the thief.

The following night, the thieves returned. The first one climbed inside and was immediately caught in a trap. "When the guards come they'll recognise me and guess that you were here too, so we shall both be killed," he told his brother. "Quick cut off my head, then nobody will know who I am and you, at least, will be safe." With a heavy heart, the second thief agreed to do as he suggested. He cut off his brother's head and took it home.

Next morning the king was astonished to find a headless man in his trap and no clue to explain what had happened. He ordered his guards to hang the man's body on the wall of the palace, and to keep watch for whoever came to take it away.

The thieves' mother was full of grief. "You must fetch your brother's body to be buried," she told the second thief, "otherwise he will wander the earth as a ghost forever."

The second thief loaded some containers of wine onto the back of a donkey and led it to the palace wall. There, he split the containers and let wine spill onto the sand. "Oh no, how can I save my wine!" he wailed loudly. The palace guards who rushed out to help couldn't resist taking a drink of the flowing wine. Before long, they had drunk so much that they fell asleep in the sun. While they slept, the thief laid his brother's body on the donkey and took it home.

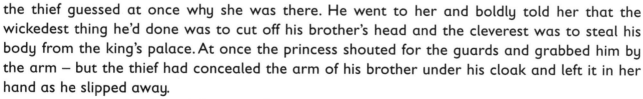

Once again, Rhampsinit discovered he had been tricked, but he was determined to catch the thief. He sent his daughter in disguise to stand outside the palace and offer herself in marriage to the cleverest and wickedest man in the kingdom. However, the thief guessed at once why she was there. He went to her and boldly told her that the wickedest thing he'd done was to cut off his brother's head and the cleverest was to steal his body from the king's palace. At once the princess shouted for the guards and grabbed him by the arm – but the thief had concealed the arm of his brother under his cloak and left it in her hand as he slipped away.

When Rhampsinit heard this story he laughed aloud, for he realised that the thief was too cunning to punish. "This thief is pardoned," he proclaimed, "for he is cleverer than us all. I shall make him my prince and he will never need to steal from my treasure house again!"

INTO THE WOODS

EUROPE
A STORY FROM GERMANY

LITTLE RED RIDING HOOD

Little Red Riding Hood loved the bright scarlet cloak that her grandmother had made her. One day she heard that Grandmother was ill, so Little Red Riding Hood put on her cloak and set off through the woods to Grandmother's house with a basket of fruit.

However, her scarlet cloak was soon spotted by the Big Bad Wolf. He stepped up beside her. "Good day, little girl," he said. "Where are you going?"

"To visit Grandmother with this basket of fruit," Little Red Riding Hood replied.

"Does she live far?" asked the Wolf.

"On the other side of the wood," Little Red Riding Hood told him, "in the cottage with the blue door."

The Wolf wished her good day and walked on. Once out of sight, he ran through the woods to the grandmother's house and knocked on the door.

"Who's there?" called Grandmother, lying in bed.

"Your granddaughter," the Wolf answered sweetly.

"Come in, dear child," said Grandmother. "The door is unlocked."

The Big Bad Wolf rushed inside, pounced on the grandmother and gobbled her up. Then he climbed into her bed, put on her nightcap and pulled the bedclothes up to his chin.

Before long, Little Red Riding Hood knocked on the door.

"Who's there?" the Wolf called weakly.

"Your granddaughter," she answered.

"Come in, dear child," replied the Wolf. "The door is unlocked."

Little Red Riding Hood entered and sat on the chair beside the bed, surprised to see how her grandmother had changed.

"What big ears you have, Grandmother," she said.

"All the better to hear you with," replied the Wolf.

"What big eyes you have, Grandmother," she said.

"All the better to see you with," the Wolf replied.

"What big teeth you have, Grandmother," said Little Red Riding Hood.

"All the better to eat you with!" cried the Wolf and he leapt out of bed and gobbled her up.

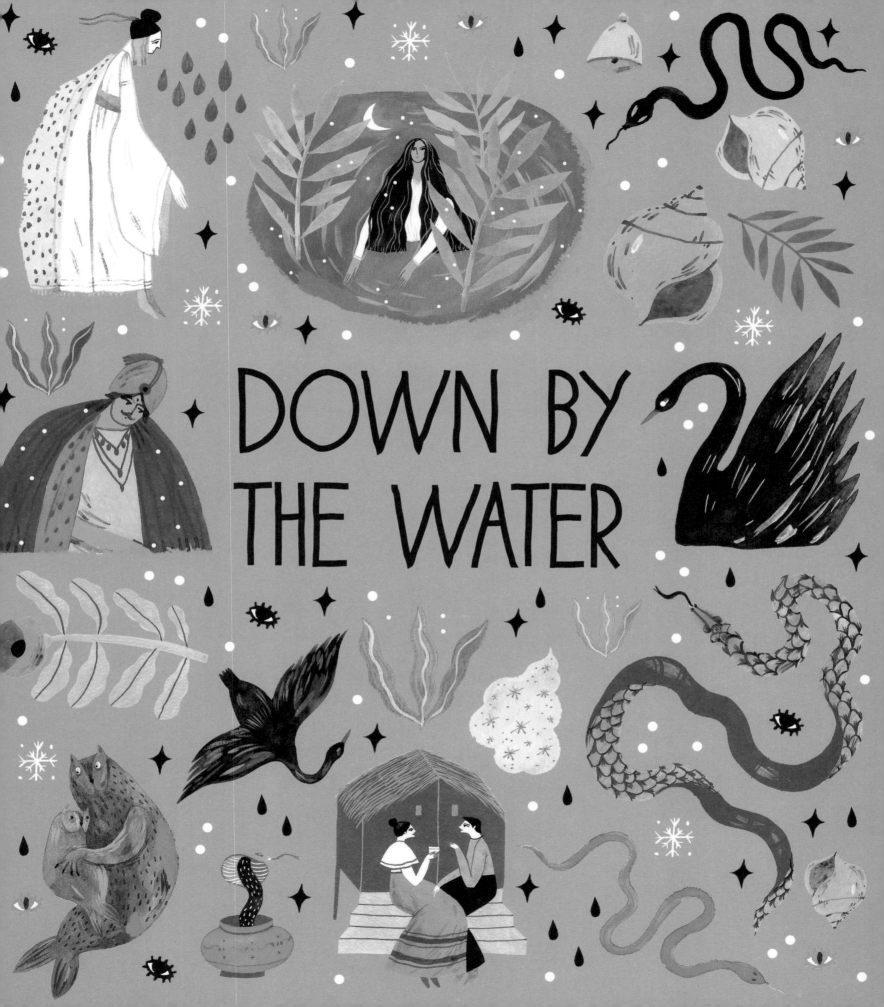

DOWN BY THE WATER

DOWN BY THE WATER

SOUTH AMERICA
A STORY FROM BRAZIL

THE STORY OF THE YARA

In a little town by a river that flowed through the rainforest, there lived a young man called Alonzo.

Alonzo was new to the country but he'd quickly grown to love the rainforest, where parrots swooped through the trees and hummingbirds darted among bright flowers. He'd also grown to love a girl called Julia and they were soon to be married.

Every day after work, Alonzo visited Julia and they sat out under the stars talking together. Afterwards, while the night was still warm, Alonzo would go to bathe in a forest pool near the river.

One evening, Alonzo told Julia about a mysterious voice he had heard singing when he went for his swim in the pool.

"It was a voice sweeter than a nightingale," he said, "but I couldn't understand the words of the song. First it came from one place and then another so I thought it must be somebody playing a trick, but when I searched among the trees and bushes there was nobody there."

At these words, Julia was filled with dread. Since childhood she'd heard tales about the fearful Yara, a forest spirit who lured young men away on the eve of their marriage. She grasped Alonzo's hands and pleaded with him not to bathe in the pool again.

"Don't worry," said Alonzo, giving her a reassuring smile. "I've been bathing in that pool for many months, there's nothing in the forest to harm me." But Julia shook her head.

"Once you have heard the song, an apparition will follow," she warned him. "And after that… your death!"

Alonzo was alarmed to see Julia tremble with fear.

"Please promise you won't return there until we are married," she urged him. "After that, the danger will be over, for I'm sure it's the voice of the Yara that you heard."

When she spoke that name, Alonzo suddenly burst into laughter with a voice wild and strange. Julia knew from the old tales that this was a sure sign he had already seen the Yara. She sank to her knees and began to weep.

Seeing her distress, Alonzo came to his senses. "Don't cry, my angel," he said, lifting her gently to his side. "I will promise anything to make you happy."

Julia thanked him but her heart was still heavy. Despite Alonzo's promise not to visit the pool by the river, she knew the song of the Yara could make men forget everything. She went into the house and returned with a beautiful shell she had kept since she was a young girl. Julia sang softly into the shell and then gave it to Alonzo.

"If you ever hear the Yara's voice," she told him, "put this to your ear and listen to my song instead. Maybe there's a chance it will be stronger than the Yara."

DOWN BY THE WATER

For three nights, Alonzo kept his promise to Julia – not because he believed the story of the Yara luring young men to their deaths, but because he knew it would make Julia cry to hear that he had visited the pool by the river.

However, the mysterious song that Alonzo had heard in the forest haunted him and, day by day, it grew stronger in his mind. At last, he could resist it no longer.

When evening came, Alonzo made his way along the forest path that led to the pool by the river. Although he'd dismissed Julia's worries, he now found himself glancing over his shoulder as he walked among the trees and bushes.

Down at the pool, Alonzo threw off his clothes and was just about to dive in when the moon appeared from behind a cloud. Suddenly, a shaft of light fell upon a beautiful woman standing among the shadowy ferns, with long hair that gleamed like the dark water.

In an instant, Alonzo grabbed his clothes and ran back down the path, crashing through the forest without daring to stop until he reached home.

Next morning, Alonzo told himself that what he'd seen had been nothing but a dream. However, the vision of the beautiful woman at the pool disturbed him all day and when he went to visit Julia that evening she noticed that he was pale and quiet.

"Don't worry, my love," he told her, "it's just a headache from the heat." But when he left Julia's house early, Alonzo didn't go home to rest; he took the path into the forest, unable to resist his desire to see the apparition again.

Alonzo reached the pool and searched for the beautiful woman but she was nowhere to be

DOWN BY THE WATER

seen, so he leaned against a tree and waited. As he gazed at the dark water, he started to feel sleepy and his limbs grew heavy. Then, before his eyes, a dim light rose from the depths of the pool, growing brighter until the waters parted and the woman appeared, her gleaming hair swirling among the waterweeds. Alonzo tried to turn away but found himself unable to flee; instead, as if in a trance, his feet were drawn towards the edge of the pool.

The Yara held out her arms to Alonzo and began to sing. Her sweet, enchanting melody drew him closer and closer, filling his mind until there was no other thought in his head.

Slowly he stepped forward, his head drooped as if sleepwalking. But as his hands fell to his sides, Alonzo's fingers brushed against Julia's shell which was in his pocket. At the same moment, his feet touched the cool water at the edge of the pool, which startled him and disturbed the Yara's trance. At once, Alonzo took the shell from his pocket. Fighting the power of the Yara's song, he raised it to his ear and heard Julia's voice.

At first Julia's song was faint, but at each note it grew louder with the strength of her love for him, until her beautiful voice seemed to fill the rainforest and was all that he could hear.

Woken from his trance, Alonzo raised his head. He was alone by an empty pool. The Yara was nowhere to be seen.

ASIA
A STORY
FROM JAPAN

DOWN BY
THE WATER

THE COLD LADY

One winter's day, a young man called Minokichi set out on a journey with his old master, Mosaku. They reached a river but were unable to cross because the ferryman had gone home, so the two travellers took shelter in the ferryman's hut.

When night came, thick snow began to fall. Despite the bitter cold, old Mosaku and Minokichi managed to fall asleep.

A few hours later, Minokichi was woken by the feeling of wet snow on his face. To his surprise, the door of the hut was open and a woman in dazzling white robes stood beside his sleeping master. The woman's skin was pale, her hair was sparkling white and icicles hung from her fingertips. She knelt down and blew a cloud of frosty breath upon old Mosaku.

After a pause, she rose and turned to Minokichi.

At once Minokichi felt an icy chill numb him to the bone. "She's going to freeze me to death!" he thought. But the Cold Lady saw that he was young and handsome and stepped away.

23

DOWN BY THE WATER

"I shall spare your life," she told him, "but you must promise never to tell anyone what you have seen; not father or mother, not wife or child, not sun, moon or stars."

Minokichi could hardly speak for the cold but he whispered a promise and then fell into a deep sleep.

In the morning, Minokichi woke to find his old master frozen to death.

Minokichi hired a cart and brought Mosaku home but he kept his promise and said nothing about what had happened that night, for fear of the Cold Lady.

Years passed. One hot summer's day, Minokichi was taking a walk when he met a pretty young girl who seemed weary with the heat. Her name was Yuki.

"I've been walking for days to find work," she explained, "but this heat makes me feel faint." Minokichi invited her to rest in his shady garden nearby, and to his delight she agreed.

When Minokichi's mother met Yuki she invited her to stay and help in the house. Yuki agreed and before the summer was over she and Minokichi had fallen in love and were married.

During the years that followed, Yuki and Minokichi had seven children, all with skin as white as jasmine flowers. Yuki worked hard but time didn't seem to age her.

One winter's evening, a snowstorm swirled outside. Yuki put the children to bed and then sat with Minokichi and began to sew by the light of a paper lantern.

As Minokichi listened to the blizzard outside and watched his wife's pale face in the lamplight, he was reminded of the mysterious encounter that happened so long ago in the ferryman's hut.

"It's strange," he said to Yuki, "this evening you remind me of a woman I met many years ago." Yuki went on sewing without looking up.

Minokichi told her how he and his master had been visited by the Cold Lady. "She killed my master with her icy breath," he said with a shiver, "then she made me promise never to tell anyone…"

Yuki looked up at him. "Not father or mother," she said, "not sister or brother, not wife or child, not sun, moon or stars."

Minokichi stared at her in disbelief.

"You've broken your promise!" Yuki cried. At once, her face turned white as snow, her hair sparkled and icicles grew at her fingertips. "I will spare your life for the sake of our children," she said, "but now I must leave you."

Then, before his eyes, Minokichi's wife vanished like a breath of frosty air.

AUSTRALIA & OCEANIA
A STORY FROM AUSTRALIA

DOWN BY THE WATER

THE BUNYIP

One hot day, in the wilderness, a group of young men set out from their camp to find food for their wives and children. Full of high spirits, they challenged each other with spear-throwing and boomerangs along the way.

After a while, they came to a valley where there was a large pool in which bulrushes were growing. Bulrush roots were good to eat but the young men didn't want to spend time wading in the water to collect them so they decided to fish instead.

All afternoon they fished without a single catch. It looked as if the young men would have to return to camp with nothing, when one of them felt a strong tug on the end of his line. "At last, a fine fish to take home to my wife," he thought and he called his friends to help him pull it out.

With one great heave they all pulled together. To their astonishment, out came a strange creature that wasn't a fish at all; it had the tail of a seal, green, scaly legs and a head with a snout like a dog. Everyone fell silent and stared, for they knew it must be the cub of the fearful Bunyip.

No sooner had they thought this than the dark water of the pool began to bubble, and the Bunyip rose from her watery den with dripping tusks and angry yellow eyes. She bellowed for her cub and the young men shuddered at the terrifying sound.

"Give her the cub!" they cried. But the man who'd caught it had promised his wife that he wouldn't return empty handed. So, despite the desperate howls of the Bunyip's mother, he lifted the creature onto his shoulders and started to run. His friends shook their spears at the Bunyip and then followed fast at his heels.

Once they'd left the pool behind, the young men were soon laughing about their adventure. However, halfway home they heard a rushing sound behind them. Looking back, they saw with alarm that the water had risen out of the Bunyip's pool and started rolling across the land

DOWN BY THE WATER

after them. They hurried on to higher ground but when they looked behind again the water had completely flooded the valley below and only the treetops could be seen.

Then they ran faster than they'd ever run before until at last they reached their camp. The young man let the Bunyip cub drop from his shoulders and everyone in the camp gathered around it, aghast. They saw the fear on the young man's face and knew at once that something terrible was happening.

"Water's coming!" he cried. "Hurry, we must climb into the trees or it will drown us."

No sooner had he said these words than water rushed in to flood the camp.

At once, the young man turned to take his wife's hand but, to his horror, a bird with black feathers, a long neck and scarlet beak stood in her place. In the same instant, his own arms turned to wings, his feet grew webs and claws and he too was transformed into a bird. The people of the camp dropped their spears and boomerangs and became a flock of black swans floating on the water.

Then the Bunyip's mother swam up to fetch her cub. When they were safely back in their den at the bottom of the bulrush pool, the floodwater slowly retreated.

However, the black swans never returned to their human form. They were left to swim in the pools and creeks and billabongs and to remember the day that one of them foolishly stole the Bunyip's cub.

DOWN BY
THE WATER

ASIA
A STORY
FROM INDIA

THE SNAKE PRINCE

Once upon a time there was an old woman who was so poor that she felt she had nothing to live for.

"I shall fetch some water from the river, for that costs nothing," she said to herself, "and after that, who knows what will become of me."

The old woman walked down to the river, taking with her a brass pot covered with a cloth to keep it clean. The day was hot and so first she bathed in the cool river. However, when she removed the cloth to fill the pot with water, inside lay the glittering coils of a deadly snake.

"Well, here's a way to end my troubles," she thought to herself and she covered up the brass pot and carried it home, intending to let a poisonous snakebite do its work. But, to her surprise, when she went to tip out the snake, a magnificent gold necklace sparkling with precious jewels tumbled onto the floor at her feet instead.

The old woman's desperation turned to joy. She wrapped the treasure in her veil and hurried off to the king's palace.

The king admired the glittering coils of the golden necklace and offered the old woman five hundred

silver pieces for it, which she gladly took. "At last my troubles are over," she thought happily and she went home.

The king gave the necklace to his wife, who was delighted with such a beautiful present. "We must keep this precious treasure safe," she said and she locked it in her jewellery chest.

A few days later, the queen decided to wear the glittering necklace at a banquet. She unlocked her jewellery chest but instead of the necklace there lay a baby boy.

The king and queen were puzzled by the mysterious baby, but as they had longed for a child for many years they welcomed it with great joy and decided to raise the boy as their own.

The old woman who had sold the necklace to the king was called back to the palace to look after the young prince.

Many happy years passed. When the prince was eighteen, he met the princess of a neighbouring kingdom and they fell in love. The night before their wedding, the princess's mother took her daughter aside. "I've heard a rumour from the prince's old nurse that there was some magic about his birth," she said. "You must find out the truth about him. Once you are married, don't speak to your husband until he tells you his secret."

The princess didn't wish for any secrets between herself and the prince, so she agreed to do as her mother suggested.

After the wedding, the princess was silent. The prince asked her what was wrong. "Dearest Husband," she replied, "I shall not speak until you tell me the secret of your birth."

The prince gazed at his wife with deep sadness in his eyes. "Please don't ask this," he said, "for if I reply, you will regret your words."

But the princess took no notice of his warning and refused to talk until the prince told her the truth.

Days and weeks passed. At last the prince could no longer bear his wife's sad silence.

"Come with me at midnight and I will answer your question," he promised, "although it breaks my heart to know that you will regret it all your life."

That night, the prince took the princess down to the river where the old woman had found the snake in the brass pot. He kissed her hands and then, with a great sigh, he spoke.

"I am the son of a king from far away," he told her. "But long ago, an enchantment turned me into a snake." As soon as the truth was spoken, the prince vanished. The princess looked about for him but all she saw was a glittering tail slip into the river and swim away. She fell to her knees and wept.

DOWN BY THE WATER

DOWN BY THE WATER

All night the princess waited in anguish for her husband to return but he never came. In the days that followed she refused to move from the spot, so a house was built for her by the riverbank, where she lived with only a few servants and guards to watch over her.

Several years passed until one morning the princess woke to find a streak of mud on the floor beside her bed. The guards assured her that nobody had entered during the night but the following morning she found the same thing again. The next night, the princess was determined to see her mysterious visitor, so she put stones under her pillow to keep herself awake.

At midnight, a snake slid into her room and laid its head upon her bed. The princess trembled with fear.

"Don't be afraid," said the snake, "I am your husband. Do you regret asking me the truth?"

"I shall regret it all my life!" cried the princess. "Isn't there anything I can do to break the spell?"

"There's only one act that can reverse the enchantment," said the snake. "Tomorrow night, place a bowl of milk and sugar in each corner of your room. All the snakes from the river will come to drink the milk, led by their queen. You must not allow them in until she promises to let you have your husband back. If you can do this, I shall be set free. But if you show any fear you shall never see me again."

The princess vowed that she would release the prince and with that he slid away.

The following evening she did exactly as he'd instructed. At midnight, to her horror, a thousand snakes swarmed out of the river, led by their glittering queen. The princess hid her terror and stood in the doorway.

"Queen of Snakes, give me back my husband," she cried. The queen swayed and flashed her dangerous eyes but the princess stood firm.

"Queen of Snakes, give me back my husband," she demanded.

The queen saw no fear in the princess, so she bowed her head. "You shall have him tomorrow," she hissed. Then the princess fainted with relief onto her bed and the snakes slithered in to drink the milk and sugar.

Next day, the princess filled the house with flowers and waited for her husband. As the Queen of Snakes had promised, the prince walked up from the river, free of his enchantment, and they were reunited at last.

When the prince and princess returned to the palace there was great rejoicing. A year later, the old woman was called to become nurse to their first child and never again did she wonder what she had to live for.

EUROPE
A STORY
FROM SCOTLAND

DOWN BY
THE WATER

MORAG AND THE WATER HORSE

Every summer, the farmers of the valleys took their cattle to graze on the lush grass that grew on the high hills.

However, Donald MacGregor wanted his cattle to have the very best grass which grew lower down the hillside, beside a deep loch. So he built his stone hut on a slip of land between the loch and a little stream that ran alongside it.

The other farmers kept away from that place because they were afraid of it. "Haven't you heard of the terrible Water Horse that lives at the bottom of the loch?" they asked Donald. "It rides up out of the water and changes its form to trick people. Then it carries them away to their doom deep down below!"

Donald just laughed. "I've no time for your tales," he scoffed. "I'll believe in the Water Horse when I meet it myself!"

"Well, you should heed our warning, Donald MacGregor," said his friends. "Build a hut on the other side of the stream and then you'll be safe, for the monster can't cross running water."

But Donald was determined that his cattle should have the best grass and paid no heed to their warnings.

One summer, his daughter Morag went up to the high hills to look after the cattle. Morag enjoyed sitting outside the hut among the heather, singing as she spun her yarn. But every evening when she walked to the loch to call in the cattle she couldn't help feeling nervous. Her father had told her there was nothing to be afraid of, but the dark water always stirred Morag's imagination with thoughts of what might lurk below.

One sunny morning, as Morag sat at her spinning wheel, a dark shadow suddenly fell upon her. She cried out in surprise. Before her stood a handsome young man with broad shoulders and long black hair.

DOWN BY THE WATER

"I'm sorry I startled you," he said with a grin.

Morag noticed that his clothes and hair were dripping with water.

"Where have you been to get so wet?" she asked.

The young man explained that he'd slipped on a narrow path beside a lake nearby and had fallen into the water. "I'll soon be dry if you let me sit here with you in the sun," he said.

Morag was pleased to have some company, so she let the young man sit on the grass beside her. Before long, she was captivated by his charm and forgot her spinning altogether. A strange look in his dark eyes made her slightly uneasy but she put the feeling out of her mind.

"Shall I comb your damp hair?" she asked.

"I'd like that," replied the young man so he laid his head upon Morag's lap and let her run a comb through his thick hair. But when Morag lifted the comb away she gasped aloud; fine threads of waterweed were wrapped around it, the same waterweed she'd once seen in her father's net when he fished in the loch. With horror she realised that the young man was the Water Horse, come to lure her away.

Morag sprang to her feet and ran for her life towards the stream. Resuming its mighty form, the Water Horse thundered after her. Just as she felt its breath on her neck, Morag leapt across the running water and fell to safety on the other side.

After his daughter's escape, Donald MacGregor never took his cattle to graze by the loch again, nor did he ever doubt any dark tale of the terrible Water Horse.

ENCHANTED PLACES

EUROPE
A STORY FROM SCOTLAND

ENCHANTED
PLACES

TAM LIN

Few people dared to walk in Carterhaugh wood for fear of an elfin knight called Tam Lin, who would take whatever he wished from those he met.

The earl who owned the wood lived in a castle nearby. When his daughter, Janet, grew up, he gave her Carterhaugh wood as a gift.

Janet was not afraid of anything. One day she decided to pick flowers and so into the wood she went.

No sooner had she picked a wild rose than handsome Tam Lin stepped out of the trees.

"Who gave you permission to pick that rose?" he asked Janet.

"I need no permission," answered Janet. "This wood belongs to me." Tam Lin looked at her and smiled. "Then you must be Janet," he said, "with whom I played when I was young."

Janet remembered a boy she had known long ago, a boy she had once loved but who had mysteriously disappeared one day. "Where have you been, Tam Lin?" she asked.

"The Fairy Queen stole me away to live with her elves under the hill," he told her. "Now I guard Carterhaugh wood as her knight but I long to escape the fairy world and return home."

"How can you be rescued?" Janet asked. "Tell me what can be done?" Tam Lin saw that she was still the brave girl he knew long ago, the brave girl he once loved.

"Tomorrow night is Halloween," he told her. "The queen and her elves will ride out across the land. If you are not afraid to wait alone at the crossroads at midnight you will see a company of knights on black steeds, followed by a company of knights on brown steeds. After them will come the Fairy Queen on a milk-white steed. I shall be riding at her side, with a star upon my crown."

"What must I do to save you?" asked Janet.

"You must pull me from my horse and hold me tight," said Tam Lin, "for the queen will use powerful magic to take me from you. If I turn into a red-hot sword you must plunge me into the river. Only then will her power be broken."

Janet promised Tam Lin with all her heart that she would be waiting at the crossroads to save him.

That Halloween night, brave Janet made her way by the eerie light of the moon to the crossroads. She hid herself and waited.

Suddenly, she heard bridles ring and hoof-beats thunder. Up rode a company of elfin knights on black steeds, followed by another company on brown steeds. After them came the Fairy Queen herself on a milk-white steed with a knight riding at her side. Janet saw the star upon his crown and without thought of her own safety, leapt forward. She seized the bridle of his horse and pulled him out of his saddle, into her arms.

At once the elves turned upon her. "Tam Lin's taken!" they cried.

The Fairy Queen shrieked and lightning flashed across the sky. Tam Lin turned into a lizard in Janet's arms but she clutched him tight. The lizard turned into a writhing snake but she held him close. The snake turned into a dove that almost flew from her grasp. Then the dove turned into a red-hot sword. Janet ran to the river nearby and plunged it in, and when the steam cleared, there lay Tam Lin, wearing his elfin robes no more. Janet wrapped him in her cloak.

The Fairy Queen scowled at Tam Lin. "I should have blinded your eyes and turned your heart to stone," she cried, and with that the whole company galloped away.

ENCHANTED PLACES

NORTH AMERICA
A STORY FROM CANADA

ENCHANTED PLACES

THE DANCE OF DEATH

There once was a girl who was beautiful and proud. She fell in love with a handsome young man from her tribe but to her annoyance he had no interest in her, for he was a great warrior, who only cared about hunting.

"Stop bothering me with talk of love," he told her sternly one day. "It's time for the autumn hunt and I must prepare."

The girl flew into a temper at his words, as she was used to having what she wanted. That evening, she called upon a secret power that had been bestowed on her by the Spirit of the Night.

The following day, when the hunters of the tribe were ready to leave, she stepped forward and stood before the young man, her eyes aflame. "Go," she cried bitterly, "but you will never return the same."

However, the young man paid no heed to her warning and set off with his brother and their companions in high spirits.

Weeks later, while hunting in the snowy forest, the young man suddenly became weak and distressed with a wild madness. His brother guessed straightaway that the girl had exercised some strange power over him. He went to the river and called upon the evil Spirit of the Stream for help.

The Spirit of the Stream was a monstrous creature. It rose out of the water with fierce eyes and terrifying horns.

"Are you afraid of me?" the Spirit asked.

The young man's brother knew that if the Spirit of the Stream found him weak he would be in great danger. "I am afraid of nothing," he answered bravely.

"Then you may ask what you wish," said the Spirit.

The brother asked for help to free the young man from the girl's wicked power.

"Take your knife and scrape a handful of powder from my horns," said the Spirit of the Stream. "Put half the powder in water for your brother to drink and give the other half to the girl, then all will be well."

ENCHANTED
PLACES

Showing no fear, the brother took his knife, grasped the monster's horns and scraped until he had a handful of powder. Then swiftly he returned to camp and prepared a cup of powder water which he gave the young man to drink.

At once the wild madness disappeared and in a few days the young man's strength returned and he was able to hunt again.

When winter ended, it was time for the hunting party to return home.

They arrived one evening to find that the annual Spring Dance was taking place in a great tent. As the night was warm, the young man's brother mixed up the rest of the powder with water and waited for the girl to come outside for a breath of air. When she did, he offered her the cup. Feeling thirsty from the dance she drank it without suspicion and then returned to the tent.

However, as she began to dance again a strange shadow suddenly came upon her. With each turn of the dance the girl rapidly aged. Her beauty faded, she began to stoop and wrinkles appeared on her face. Everyone stopped and stared but the girl danced on, unaware that she was growing old before their eyes.

"See her hands tremble," people whispered. "Look at her faltering feet. It is the Dance of Death!"

On and on she danced, tottering unsteadily as her life ebbed away until, withered by old age, she stumbled and fell at the feet of the young man.

Her dance was over. The evil Spirit of the Stream had done its work and she could trouble the young man no more.

EUROPE
A STORY
FROM WALES

ENCHANTED
PLACES

THE LADY OF THE LAKE

High among the Black Mountains lies the lake of Llyn y Fan Fach.

One summer's day, a young farmer named Gwyn brought his cattle to graze on the sweet grass beside the lake. As he sat, gazing across the water, out of it rose a beautiful young woman. Gwyn stared in wonder. He'd never seen such a perfect vision and in a heartbeat he loved her.

She stepped slowly across the water.

Gwyn was lost for words. All he could offer her was a dry crust of bread from his pocket.

The Lady of the Lake shook her head.

"I shall not be yours for dry bread," she said and she sank back into the water.

Gwyn returned to the lake the following day, desperate to see her again. This time he brought a soft loaf.

The Lady of the Lake appeared as before, but wouldn't accept his gift. "I shall not be yours for soft bread," she told him and she descended into the water once more.

That night, Gwyn baked the perfect loaf.

Next day, when the Lady of the Lake came to him she smiled with loving eyes. "I shall be yours for this perfect loaf," she said and she stepped out of the water to his side.

Gwyn pledged his heart to the Lady of the Lake and asked her to marry him.

"I will marry you, Gwyn, and I foresee we'll be happy," she replied. "But if you strike me three times I will have to leave you."

"That I will never do," promised Gwyn. "I would rather cut off my hand than use it to strike you."

Then the Lady of the Lake called for her cattle and a herd of fine beasts stepped out of the water. They joined Gwyn's own herd and he led them all down the mountain to his home in the village below.

Gwyn and the Lady of the Lake were wed and lived happily as she had foreseen. As time passed they had three sons and although Gwyn aged with the years, his wife's beauty never faded.

All was well until, one day, the family attended a christening. During the service, to Gwyn's surprise, his wife began to laugh out loud. He tapped her on the arm.

"Hush," he said. "What makes you laugh?"

"I foresee happiness for the parents of this child," she replied. "But that is the first strike, Husband, take care!"

Gwyn promised her it would never happen again.

ENCHANTED PLACES

All was well until, one day, the family went to a wedding. During the service, to Gwyn's surprise, his wife began to cry. Once again he tapped her on the arm.

"Dry your tears," he said. "What makes you cry?"

"I foresee trouble in this marriage," she replied. "And that was the second strike, Husband, take care!"

Gwyn promised her with all his heart that it wouldn't happen a third time.

All was well until, one day, the family went to a funeral. During the service, to Gwyn's surprise, his wife began to laugh. Once again he tapped her on the arm.

"Sshh!" he said. "What makes you laugh?"

"I foresee rest for this poor soul after long years of suffering," she replied. "But that was the third strike, Husband, so I must leave you."

Gwyn was heartbroken. He followed his wife and pleaded with her to stay, but the Lady of the Lake called for her cattle and walked back up the mountain. There, she stepped into the lake and vanished.

The three sons often saw their mother when they visited the lake of Llyn y Fan Fach but Gwyn never set eyes on his beloved wife again.

EUROPE
A STORY FROM FRANCE

ENCHANTED PLACES

THE WATER WITCH

Wililliam was a poor cowherd who loved a dairymaid called Bella. One day, he decided to give up work on the farm to seek his fortune. "I shall come home with my pockets full of gold so that we can be married," he promised Bella.

Bella didn't want William to go but he was determined. When it was time for him to leave, Bella fetched three things that her father had given her before he died. The first was a little bell which could be heard by a friend in time of danger. The second was a knife which had the power to undo any enchantment and the third was a staff which would take its owner wherever they wanted to go.

Bella gave William the bell and the knife. "I shall keep the staff," she said and with a heavy heart she wished him good luck.

William set off over the mountains. After a couple of days he came to a village beside a lake, where he overheard two men talking about a Water Witch. William asked them who she was.

"She's a fairy creature who lives at the bottom of the lake," they told him, "and she's richer than all the kings and queens together. Many people have gone to her palace hoping for riches but none have ever returned."

"Maybe the Water Witch will give me just enough gold to fill my purse so that I can marry Bella," thought William. He went down to the lake where a boat in the shape of a swan appeared.

The swan boat carried William into the middle of the lake, then it plunged below the surface to a crystal palace surrounded by a garden of water lilies. A voice called William to enter.

The Water Witch lay on a golden couch. Her long hair gleamed with the blues and greens of a dragonfly and her skin was as fine as pearl. She welcomed William and served him the most delicious wine he had ever tasted. Then she asked if he would like to see her treasure chambers.

William gasped in amazement as they walked through rooms piled high with gold and jewels, but the Water Witch seemed sad.

"It's so lonely here," she told him. "Half of this could be yours if you would stay with me and be my husband."

Dazzled by the riches before him and overcome by the enchanted wine he had drunk, William forgot all about Bella and agreed to marry the Water Witch without hesitation.

ENCHANTED PLACES

The Water Witch smiled and promised to prepare him a feast. She went into her garden where there stood a large fish tank.

"Come, Baker!" she called. "Come, Butcher! Come, Blacksmith!" Three little fish swam to the surface and she scooped them up in a silver fishing net. The Water Witch carried them into her kitchen and began to cook them on the stove.

Suddenly, William thought he heard the fish whispering.

"What's that sound?" he asked.

"Just butter hissing in the frying pan," replied the Water Witch.

Then William heard the fish crying.

"What's that sound?" he asked.

"Only birds of the lake calling" replied the Water Witch.

Then William heard the fish shout out loud.

"What's that sound?" he asked.

"Nothing but wood crackling on the fire," replied the Water Witch.

When the fish were served, the Water Witch went to fetch William another glass of wine. While she was gone, he took out the knife Bella had given him. As soon as it touched the fish they became little men.

"Save yourself!" cried the Baker, the Butcher and the Blacksmith. "We came here to get rich but the Water Witch turned us into fish and she'll do the same to you too."

William jumped up to escape but at that moment the Water Witch returned and saw that he'd discovered her plan. She struck him with her silver fishing net, turning him into a frog and then tossed him into the fish tank.

As William tumbled through the water, the little bell which was around his neck rang out.

Far, far away, Bella heard the sound of the bell and knew that William was in danger.

She fetched the staff her father had given her and cried, "Take me to William!" The staff became a horse and Bella climbed on its back. It galloped swiftly until they reached a mountain.

"Take me to William!" she cried and the horse became an eagle, which flew her up to the mountaintop.

On the top of the mountain, Bella found a Dwarf chained to a rock. "Please save me," the Dwarf cried.

"I've come to save my dear William," said Bella.

"If magic has brought you to me then you must need my help," said the Dwarf. "It was my wife, the wicked Water Witch, who left me chained here; William must also be in her power. To rescue us you must go the witch's palace and catch her in her silver fishing net."

"Thank you," said Bella. "I promise I shall save you both." She told the eagle to take her to William and it carried her to the lake of the Water Witch.

Bella made her way to the Water Witch's palace just as William had done, and received the same welcome. While the Water Witch went to fetch some wine, Bella noticed her father's knife on the table so she hid it in her jacket pocket.

When the Water Witch returned, Bella admired her silver fishing net. "How beautiful, may I fish with it?" she asked.

The Water Witch wanted to entice her guest to stay, so she agreed. Without suspicion, she handed Bella the net.

At once, Bella swung the net over the Water Witch. There was a terrifying howl and she turned into a huge, ugly fish. At once Bella scooped her up and tipped her into the fish tank.

Then up swam the frog with her father's bell around his neck. Bella lifted him out and gently touched his foot with the knife. To her joy, William's enchantment was broken. When he explained what had happened, Bella released all the men who'd been turned into fish.

As soon as his wife lost her power, the Dwarf's chains vanished and he returned to the palace. To thank Bella and William he filled their pockets with gold.

"Now take us home," Bella told her father's staff happily. "We have a wedding to arrange!"

ENCHANTED PLACES

ASIA

A STORY

FROM CHINA

ENCHANTED
PLACES

THE MAIDEN
IN THE PAGODA

Long ago, among the ancient ruins of Luoyang, stood a towering pagoda that rose a hundred storeys high.

One summer's day, a maiden who lived nearby was sitting in the shady courtyard of her family home when the sky suddenly grew dark. She jumped up and ran towards the house but before she reached the door, a magic whirlwind lifted her high into the air and carried her away.

When the maiden opened her eyes she found herself inside the topmost room of the pagoda. A handsome young man stood beside her.

"It seems that heaven has brought us together," he said with a bow. "If you promise to marry me I will give you everything your heart desires."

The maiden was afraid. "No I won't marry you," she answered. "I want to go home."

"If you won't marry me then you'll stay here until you change your mind," the young man replied. He set a table with bread and wine, locked the windows and left the maiden alone. As he descended the stairs he removed some of the steps above him so that she couldn't escape.

Next day, the young man returned with silk dresses and embroidered slippers. "These are the finest in the land," he said.

The maiden had never seen such beautiful clothes but she would not change her mind and agree to marry him.

The following day the young man brought a huge ruby gemstone which shone brightly and lit the pagoda at night. Still, he received the same answer.

Day after day, the young man came. He brought gifts of delicious food, painted fans, and precious jewels. The maiden had all her heart could desire and yet she was not happy.

One day, the maiden noticed that the young man had forgotten to lock the windows before he left. Cautiously, she peeped out. To her horror, she saw a hideous, winged ogre climb onto the window ledge below. His wild hair was as red as blood, his eyes bulged out of their sockets and crooked fangs jutted from his ugly mouth. With a grunt the ogre leapt from the pagoda and flew to the ground, where at once he changed into the young man and hurried away.

The maiden was seized with terror. How could she escape the monster who had imprisoned her? Looking down, she saw a woodcutter far below. The maiden waved and called frantically, but the old man didn't see or hear her.

Thinking quickly, the maiden grabbed the old clothes she had exchanged for the ogre's fine silk dresses and threw them out of the window. Her only hope of help, they fluttered down from a hundred storeys high and fell at the woodcutter's feet.

The woodcutter gathered the clothes and gazed up at the pagoda. All he could see was a tiny figure so high she was almost in the clouds. What could it mean? Shaking his head at the mystery he carried on his way.

The maiden wept with despair.

But that night, the woodcutter remembered that his neighbour's daughter had been carried away by a magic storm. Next morning he took the clothes to her parents, who were overjoyed when they recognised them. At once, the maiden's brother picked up his axe and vowed he would bring her home.

As the maiden's brother approached the pagoda, the young man came along the path. Before his eyes, the young man become an ogre once more and spread his wings to take flight. Without a moment's hesitation, the brother threw his axe and struck off one of the wings. With a roar of fury the ogre clutched his shoulder and fled to the hills.

From her high window, the maiden watched the ogre disappear into the forest with tears of relief. Then her brother climbed the stairs to the top of the pagoda to set her free.

ENCHANTED PLACES

AFRICA
A STORY FROM WEST AFRICA

ENCHANTED PLACES

THE TALKING SKULL

There once was a hunter who went into a forest. Among the shadows at the foot of a tree he noticed a human skull. The hunter was about to walk quickly on when, to his astonishment, the skull spoke to him.

"What are you doing in this lonely place?" asked the skull.

"I'm hungry," said the hunter. "I'm looking for food."

"Hmm," muttered the skull. "I can tell you where to find some fruit if you can keep a quiet tongue in your head."

The hunter agreed, so the skull told him where to find delicious fruit growing nearby.

The hunter thanked the skull. "Tell me," he asked, "what killed you at the foot of that tree?"

"Too much talking," replied the skull. The hunter was puzzled by this reply but the skull would say no more.

When he got back to his village, the hunter decided to tell his chief about the talking skull, thinking he would receive a handsome reward for such news.

As he guessed, the chief was very keen to have a talking skull. "Such a marvel would bring me great fame," thought the chief, so he sent two warriors with the hunter to fetch it.

When they reached the forest, the hunter found the skull once more. "Speak," demanded the warriors, but the skull didn't make a sound.

"Speak, friend!" said the hunter, but the skull remained silent.

This made the warriors angry. "You've made a fool of us and our chief," they cried and they cut off the hunter's head and left it lying beside the skull.

When they'd gone, the skull spoke. "So, what brought you here, to the foot of this tree?" it asked.

The hunter's head sighed. "Too much talking," he replied.

STRANGERS AT THE DOOR

EUROPE
A STORY
FROM FRANCE

STRANGERS AT THE DOOR

THE ENCHANTED APPLE TREE

Long ago, the sweetest apples in France grew on a tree that belonged to a very grumpy woman.

Nothing ever pleased her except her apple tree and nothing made her grumpier than people reaching over her garden fence to pick the apples. Whenever she caught them she chased them away with a broom.

Because of this she was known as 'Old Misery'.

One day, a man with a long white beard knocked on Misery's door.

"Could you kindly spare me an apple from your tree?" he asked. "They are such a rosy red, I'm sure they must be the sweetest in France."

Misery was pleased that somebody had asked her permission for once, and with such politeness too, so she picked him an apple. "It will be the best you've ever tasted," she promised him proudly.

The stranger thanked her. "As you've been kind enough to share with me," he said, "I shall grant you a wish."

Misery thought for a moment and then smiled. "I wish that anybody who touches one of my apples will stick to the tree until I let them go!" she said.

"So it shall be promised," said the stranger and he went on his way.

The following morning, two boys reached over the fence to pick some apples and found themselves stuck to the tree. No matter how much they tugged and twisted, they couldn't pull themselves free.

"Aha!" said Misery. "That serves you right for not asking my permission." She made the boys promise never to touch her tree again before she released them.

The next day, Misery found a farmer, a baker and a goat stuck to her tree. All of them got a good telling-off before she let them go free.

Years passed. Misery and her apple tree both became old and bent.

One day, an ancient figure appeared at her door. Misery recognized at once that it was Father Death.

"I'm not ready to go with you yet, old man," she complained.

"It's no use arguing, Misery," said Father Death. "When I call, you must come."

Misery thought for a moment, then she nodded her head.

"As you wish," she said. "But let me pack a basket of food for us to share on our journey. I shall slice some bread and cheese if you will fetch us two delicious apples from the tree in my garden. I'm so bent now that I can't reach the best fruit anymore."

Father Death had never been offered such a kindness before. He went into Misery's garden and reached up high for an apple, but when he touched the tree he became stuck to it.

STRANGERS AT THE DOOR

Father Death cried out in rage. He tugged and twisted but he couldn't pull himself free. "Get me down, Misery!" he demanded. "You can't keep me here!"

"Don't make such a noise, old man," she scolded. "You shall stay there until I'm ready to go with you." And, despite his angry shouts, Misery left Father Death hanging in the tree.

Years went by and while Father Death remained stuck to the apple tree nobody died. He couldn't end the suffering of those in pain, he couldn't offer rest to the elderly who were weary of living, and this caused much unhappiness in the world.

Eventually, Father Death called for Misery to make a bargain. "Release me from your apple tree," he said, "and I promise that you won't have to come with me until you want to."

Misery smiled with satisfaction at this bargain and released her prisoner.

However, she is still not ready to go with Father Death, so that is why you can find Misery in the world today.

EUROPE
A STORY
FROM RUSSIA

STRANGERS AT THE DOOR

THE BLACKSMITH AND THE DEMON

A blacksmith went to church one day, where a painting caught his eye. At the top of the picture sat God on his throne and at the bottom was the Devil at his fiery furnace.

The Blacksmith stared at it thoughtfully. "I say my prayers to God every day," he said to himself, "so I ought to show respect to the Devil."

When he returned home, he painted the Devil on the door of his workshop. Each morning, before entering the workshop, he wished the Devil "Good Day".

When the Blacksmith died, his son took over his trade. However, the young Blacksmith saw no reason to show respect to the Devil. Instead, each morning he thumped him on the head with his hammer.

Before long, the Devil grew tired of these insults.

One day, the Devil came to the workshop, disguised as a young man looking for a job. The Blacksmith had plenty of work so he took him on as his apprentice.

The Blacksmith was amazed at how fast his apprentice learned to use the hammer and tongs at the fiery furnace. Very soon, the apprentice showed more skill than his master.

While the Blacksmith was away on business one day, the apprentice noticed an old lady driving by in her carriage. He rushed outside and began to shout.

"Age becomes youth!" he cried. "We turn old folks into young ones!" When she heard this the old lady told her coachman to stop.

"How much does it cost?" she asked the apprentice.

"Five hundred roubles," he replied. Thinking it was a bargain, she gave him the money.

The apprentice sent the coachman to buy two buckets of milk which he tipped into a barrel. Then he grabbed the old woman by her feet and flung her into the furnace. When the fire had burned down, he picked out her bones with his tongs and dropped them into the barrel of milk.

To the coachman's amazement, out stepped a beautiful young woman who clapped her hands with delight.

STRANGERS AT THE DOOR

When she returned home the young woman's husband didn't recognise her.

"The Blacksmith's apprentice restored my youth," she told him. "Go and ask him to do the same for you."

The husband agreed to do as she wished. However, when he got to the workshop the apprentice had left and the Blacksmith, who had returned from his business, was there alone.

"Make me young again, like my wife," said the husband and he offered the Blacksmith five hundred roubles.

The Blacksmith laughed. "I can't do that!" he said.

"Well, my coachman saw your apprentice do it," insisted the husband, "and he must have learned it from you, so please do as I ask."

The Blacksmith eyed the five hundred roubles. He asked the coachman to describe what the apprentice had done. As it seemed to have worked, he agreed to do the same for the husband.

The coachman fetched two buckets of milk and the Blacksmith threw the husband into the furnace. But when he put the husband's bones in the barrel of milk, nothing happened. They waited all day, but the bones just lay at the bottom of the barrel.

The coachman hurried home to report this news to his mistress, who had the Blacksmith hauled off to prison and thrown in a dungeon.

Confused and alone, the Blacksmith thought nothing could help him, until his apprentice appeared.

"I can save you," said the apprentice, "but you must respect the Devil on your door from now on."

The Blacksmith promised he would never strike the Devil with his hammer again. Then the apprentice went to the workshop and returned with the husband, as young as the day he was wed.

NORTH AMERICA
A PASSAMAQUODDY STORY

STRANGERS AT THE DOOR

THE GIRL AND THE CHENOO

Autumn was the time for young men to make their annual hunting trip to the forest to get food and skins for their people.

One year, three brothers asked their sister to join them. They set out in canoes along the river, deep into the forest. When they found a good place to camp they built a wigwam covered with bark, to be their home over the winter months.

Each day, while the three brothers were out hunting, their sister gathered berries, collected firewood and prepared a stew in the cooking pot for their return. After the meal, they sat around the fire and shared the day's adventures. The girl loved to hear her brothers' stories about moose and bears and mountain lions but she never had a brave tale of her own to match theirs.

Then, one evening, the brothers returned with fear in their eyes. Each one had seen the footprints of a huge beast, which had filled their hearts with dread.

However, a good dinner around the cheery fire soon had them laughing at their fears.

"Those tracks must have been made by a bear," the first brother decided, and the others were quick to agree. "Of course," they said, "there's no other explanation."

But their sister said nothing, for she too had seen the tracks while she'd been collecting firewood and knew that such huge footprints could only belong to the giant Chenoo – a fierce creature from the cold northlands who had once been a man but whose wickedness had turned his heart to ice. She was afraid to even speak his name aloud, for the Chenoo ate people without mercy.

"He will see the smoke from our fire," thought the girl. "I must be ready."

Next morning, when her brothers had gone, she quickly gathered a basket of berries and cooked up a big stew. Then she put the bearskins they slept on into a pile, opened the door of the wigwam and sat beside it to wait.

She didn't have to wait long before the ground shook with heavy footsteps and out of the trees lumbered the monstrous Chenoo, a manlike creature with leathery skin, shaggy hair and wolfish eyes. The girl was struck with terror but she hid her fear and greeted him with a smile.

"Welcome, Grandfather," she said. "I'm so glad that you've come to visit us. I have cooked a meal for you."

The Chenoo stood before her, taken by surprise at this kind greeting, for people usually screamed when he appeared. He smelt the delicious stew wafting from the wigwam and saw the basket of berries inside.

"Granddaughter," he said in a voice that boomed like thunder in the mountains, "I will eat your meal." So she led him inside.

There was just enough space for the huge Chenoo to sit in the wigwam. He ate the stew in one gulp, followed by the berries in a mouthful. Then he eyed the girl. She trembled, fearing that the Chenoo would eat her next, but he didn't move.

"Granddaughter," he said, "because you

have welcomed me as your Grandfather I shall not devour you."

Then the girl offered him water to wash himself. "You look tired from travelling, Grandfather," she said gently. "Let me spread out these bearskins for you to rest."

The Chenoo groaned deeply. "It's true, Granddaughter, I am tired," he said and when she'd spread the bearskins across the floor of the wigwam, he lay down and fell asleep.

That evening, the brothers returned in high spirits, bringing rabbits, a goose and a fine deer they had caught, but their sister greeted them with a silent warning. Then she spoke.

"Welcome home, brothers," she said loudly. "I have good news. Our grandfather has come to visit." At that moment the wigwam shook and the gruesome face of the Chenoo appeared at the doorway. The brothers stared in horror, but to their astonishment their sister seemed unafraid.

"Brothers, welcome our grandfather," she said calmly.

The brothers hid their fear. "Forgive us, Grandfather," they stuttered, "we didn't

STRANGERS AT THE DOOR

recognise you."

"Because you have greeted me as your grandfather and brought food for my dinner I shall not eat you," said the Chenoo and he grabbed the rabbits, the goose and the deer and gulped them down one by one.

The brothers could only watch aghast but their sister explained to the Chenoo that they now had no food for their own dinner. "Can you help us, Grandfather?" she asked.

"Whatever you wish, Granddaughter," replied the Chenoo and with a giant stride he tramped off through the trees.

Before the girl could tell her brothers all that had happened that day, the Chenoo returned, carrying a large moose in either hand.

That evening the girl cooked a great feast. Then, as there was only room in the wigwam for the Chenoo to sleep, the others wished their grandfather goodnight and settled on the ground outside, although none of them slept at all.

Next morning, however, the Chenoo built himself a huge wigwam nearby and from that day on, he helped the brothers hunt the finest game. Before long they had learned not to fear him and by the time spring arrived they had gathered plenty of food and skins to take back to their people.

Eventually, it was time to leave the forest.

"I wish to come with you, my grandchildren," said the Chenoo.

"But our people are afraid of you, Grandfather," the girl told him.

"Then build me a sweat lodge," said the Chenoo, "and put in plenty of hot stones from the fire."

When this was done, the creature from the cold northlands shut himself inside.

Three times the Chenoo asked for more hot stones until, at last, the door opened and out stepped an old man with a white beard. He put his hand to his mouth and coughed out a tiny piece of ice, shaped like a man.

"Granddaughter," he said, "your kindness has melted the wickedness in me. Throw this heart of ice onto the fire." Gladly she did his bidding and the heart of ice melted away.

Then the three brothers and their sister took their grandfather home, where they lived happily together for many years.

STRANGERS AT THE DOOR

EUROPE
A STORY FROM IRELAND

THE HORNED WOMEN

STRANGERS AT
THE DOOR

Late one evening, a lady sat at her fireside combing wool to prepare it for spinning, while her family slept upstairs.

Suddenly there was an urgent knock at the door. "Open, open!" a voice cried.

Thinking that a neighbour was in trouble the lady opened the door, but there stood a woman in black robes with a horn on her head, carrying a pair of carding combs.

The lady was seized with fear. "Who are you?" she asked.

"I am the Mountain Witch of the One Horn," replied the stranger and without waiting to be invited, she hurried inside, sat herself by the fire and began at once to comb the wool.

Before the lady could question her there was a second knock on the door and she felt herself strangely compelled to open it. There stood a woman with two horns on her head, carrying a spinning wheel.

"I am the Mountain Witch of the Two Horns," the woman said and she walked right in, sat down at her spinning wheel and began to spin the wool to make yarn.

Ten more witches arrived at the house, each with one horn more than the one before, so that the last had twelve horns upon her head. They all sat round the fire, busily combing wool, spinning yarn and weaving it into cloth. As they worked they murmured a bewitching rhyme and the lady of the house found herself spellbound, unable to move or cry out for help.

After a while, the Witch of the one Horn called for her to make them a cake.

"I'll need water from the well," said the lady.

"Then fetch it in a sieve," instructed the witch.

The lady took her sieve outside to the well but she knew that the witches had given her an impossible task. No matter how she tried, the water ran right through it. Afraid to return without any water, she sat down by the well and wept.

The Spirit of the Well heard the lady's tears and spoke from the deep, dark water below. "Stand at the north corner of the house and cry aloud that the sky above the mountain is red with fire," she said.

The lady thanked the Spirit of the Well and cried out loud as she was told. The witches heard her words and shrieked with horror.

"Our home is ablaze!" they screamed rushing out of the house and they flew off into the night.

"When the witches realise they've been tricked, they are sure to return," warned the Spirit of the Well. She told the lady to sprinkle water that she'd used to wash her children's feet across the doorstep, then take the cloth the witches had woven and place it half in and half out of a chest with a padlock. Lastly, she told the lady to secure the door by wedging a great wooden beam across it so that the witches couldn't enter.

Sure enough, it wasn't long before the twelve horned witches returned, furious at having been tricked. They hammered on the door.

"Open, open, feetwater!" they demanded.

"I cannot," said the feetwater. "I am scattered across the doorstep and can only run down to the lake."

"Open, open, woven cloth!" they demanded.

"I cannot," said the cloth. "I am trapped in a locked chest."

"Open, open, wood of the door!" they demanded.

"I cannot," said the door. "A beam is wedged tight across me."

Then the twelve horned witches cursed the Spirit of the Well who had defeated them and flew back to their mountain.

Safe from harm, the lady of the house never saw her unwelcome guests again.

STRANGERS AT THE DOOR

ASIA
A KOREAN STORY

STRANGERS AT THE DOOR
THE BLIND MAN AND THE DEMONS

A blind fortune-teller was stopped one day by an errand boy who asked him the way to a house.

"I have to deliver a box from the baker," explained the boy. "If only you could see, it's full of beautiful coloured cakes."

The blind fortune-teller couldn't see the cakes, but he had a supernatural power which enabled him to see evil demons and he saw a crowd of wicked demons of many colours, hovering above the box.

The blind man knew those demons would cause trouble once they entered a house, so he gave the boy directions and then followed him and waited nearby.

Sure enough, not long after the errand boy had delivered the cakes, there were cries of alarm in the house. A servant ran out in tears. She told the blind man that the daughter of the house had suddenly died.

"Tell your master that I can save her," said the blind fortune-teller. "I saw evil demons enter your house and I have the power to catch them."

When the master of the house heard this he invited the blind man inside.

The blind fortune-teller set to work in the small room where the girl was lying. First, he closed the doors and windows tightly. Then he pasted paper over all the cracks in the walls so that not even a speck of light could pass through. When this was done, he sat by the girl and began to mutter a magical chant.

As the fortune-teller had foreseen, the evil demons had entered the girl's body. When they heard his magic words they began to moan and groan, wanting to get away. They made such a terrifying noise that a servant poked a hole in one of the papered-up cracks to see what was happening.

As soon as the demons knew there was a way of escape they flew out of the girl's body, swooped through the hole the servant had made and rushed away. The girl quickly recovered and her father thanked the blind

STRANGERS AT
THE DOOR

fortune-teller, offering him many gifts.

But the blind fortune-teller sadly shook his head. "I shall not live long, now," he said. "As I failed to capture those evil demons, they will take their revenge on me."

Shortly afterwards, the king heard about the fortune-teller's supernatural powers and decided to test him to find out if the blind man really could see. He called for him to be brought to the palace, and put a rat in a cage before him.

"What can you see, blind man?" asked the king.

"Three rats, Your Majesty," answered the blind fortune-teller.

"Wrong!" cried the king. "You have no supernatural powers, you are nothing more than a trickster who has deceived my people."

The blind fortune-teller insisted that he saw the truth. But the king ordered him to be put to death for lying and he was taken away from the palace to the place of execution.

When the fortune-teller had gone, one of the courtiers noticed that the rat was behaving strangely. He took her to the king and before their eyes she gave birth to two babies.

"The blind man did see the truth!" exclaimed the king in wonder. "Stop the execution."

A guard ran to the top of the watchtower where a flag was kept to give instructions to the executioner; waving it to the left would signal death to the prisoner. Waving it to the right would spare his life. The guard seized the flag and tried to wave it to the right, but a sudden gust of evil wind blew it hard to the left.

"Revenge!" screamed the demons and the blind fortune-teller was executed.

ASIA
A STORY FROM SYRIA

STRANGERS AT THE DOOR

THE CLEVER GOLDSMITH

There once was a goldsmith whose skill was known far and wide.

One day, a stranger in black robes appeared at the window of the goldsmith's shop. When the stranger entered, the room was filled with shadows.

"I am the Prince of Darkness," he said. "I wish to have everything that is in your window."

The goldsmith nodded nervously. "Of course, it is all yours, my lord," he replied.

"Then promise to keep it safe for me," said the Prince of Darkness. "I shall return for it when I'm ready."

The goldsmith promised and his grim customer left.

Moments later, the goldsmith noticed his young daughter, Zorah, playing in the window. With horror, he realised that he had promised her to the Prince of Darkness.

Years passed without another visit from the Prince of Darkness. However, when Zorah was seventeen, he finally returned.

Zorah was away that day, visiting her grandmother. The goldsmith offered the Prince of Darkness all the fine jewellery in his workshop but he only wanted Zorah for his queen.

"I shall be back in seven days to fetch what's mine," he said.

The goldsmith lost no time. He made hundreds of tiny cogs and wheels and then he bought a large quantity of wax.

When the Prince of Darkness returned, the goldsmith presented him with a lifelike mechanical model of Zorah.

"Here is my daughter," said the goldsmith. "She is honoured to be your queen."

The Prince of Darkness took his bride to his cold kingdom, where a fire had been prepared to welcome her.

But, to his surprise, when she sat before the fire his queen melted right away.

"Ha!" roared the Prince of Darkness. "I see these humans are too soft to live in my kingdom. I shall have nothing more to do with them!"

And the clever goldsmith never saw him again.

IN FARM AND FIELD

EUROPE
A STORY FROM ENGLAND

IN FARM AND FIELD

YALLERY BROWN

One evening, a young farmhand called Tom was walking home across the fields when he heard someone sobbing.

"That sounds like a child," he thought to himself. He looked over the hedge and down the lane but he couldn't see anybody.

Then the voice cried out again. "Oh, this stone! This stone is so heavy on me!"

Tom gazed around and saw a large flat stone beneath the hedge. He lifted the heavy stone up and there, lying in a hole was the strangest little figure Tom had ever seen. He was no bigger than a baby but he had the wrinkled brown face of an old man, with long yellow hair and a long yellow beard wrapped around his body.

Tom stared in amazement.

The little man jumped to his feet. "Yallery Brown," he said with a bow. "You're a good lad and you've done me a great favour. Now I must do you a favour in return. Maybe you'd like some help with your work?"

Tom, who was lazy by nature, liked this idea. "Well, if you could give me a helping hand," he said, "then I'll thank—"

"Stop!" cried Yallery Brown. "You mustn't thank me, for I promise if you do you'll never see me again!" Then he wished Tom goodnight, spun around on the spot and vanished into thin air.

Next morning, Tom thought that what he'd seen and heard had been a dream. But when he arrived at the farm, the horses had been fed, the stables swept, and all of his other work was done. Yallery Brown had been true to his word.

And so it continued in the days that followed. Tom never saw his helper but every job the farmer gave him was done by invisible hands. Tom was delighted to be paid without having to do any work!

However, before long, things began to go wrong at the farm. Whatever job was done for Tom was undone for the other farm hands. If his horse was groomed, theirs was

IN FARM
AND FIELD

splashed with mud. If his bucket was filled with water, theirs was overturned. If his tools were sharpened, theirs were made blunt. It wasn't long before they became suspicious of Tom and stopped speaking to him.

Tom realised that Yallery Brown's help was full of mischief.

"I shall have to do my own work," he decided. But that was not so easy. When he picked up a broom it slid out of his hand. When he took hold of the plough it ran away from him. Tom wished that he'd never listened to the voice under the stone.

Eventually, Yallery Brown caused so much trouble meddling at the farm that Tom lost his job. In despair, he went out to the field and called for Yallery Brown.

Yallery Brown appeared with a wicked glint in his eye.

"I don't want your help any more," Tom told him crossly. "You've only caused me trouble and I'll thank you to leave me alone!"

Then Yallery Brown laughed with glee. "I told you not to thank me," he cried. "Now I won't help you and you shan't see me again. But I never promised to leave you alone!" And he began to sing…

"Work hard as you will,

You'll never do well.

Work hard as you may,

You'll earn no pay.

For harm and mischief and Yallery Brown

You let out yourself from under the stone!"

Then he danced away, chuckling to himself.

From that day on, nothing went well for Tom his whole life long – for there was no end to the harm and mischief of Yallery Brown.

EUROPE
A STORY FROM NORWAY

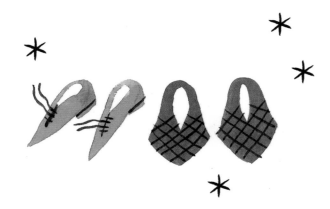

OLD NICK AND THE GIRL

IN FARM AND FIELD

I n a town beside a lake, there lived a girl who loved dancing more than anything. She danced in the house, she danced in the fields and wherever a fiddle was playing she would be there, whirling and spinning and kicking her heels.

But although the girl was light and fast on her feet she only had shoes made of birch bark. "I wish I could dance in a pair of leather shoes with a good spring in the sole," she sighed to herself. "With shoes like that my feet would hardly touch the ground."

Her wish was overheard by Old Nick, a devil who was always looking for the chance to lead someone astray…

One morning, the girl was gazing longingly at the shoe stall in the market when Old Nick came up beside her and asked what she was thinking.

"I'm wondering how I can get some leather shoes to dance in," she replied, "for I have no money to buy them."

"Maybe I can help you," said Old Nick and he produced a pair of beautiful red leather shoes. "Do you like these?"

The girl took the shoes and stroked their soft leather, marvelling at their fine stitches and strong, sturdy soles. "Is there a spring in them?" she asked.

"Try them for yourself," said Old Nick.

When the girl put the shoes on they fitted perfectly. She skipped a little and then kicked her heels and felt such a spring in her step that she laughed aloud. "Oh, I could dance all day and all night in these!" she sighed.

Old Nick smiled. "If you want them, maybe we could come to some agreement," he said.

The girl couldn't bear to part with the shoes and was determined to have them so, despite not having any money to pay for them, she began to bargain with Old Nick. At last it was

decided that she could have the shoes for a whole year without any payment as long as she would dance for Old Nick when the year was out.

IN FARM AND FIELD

"If you're not satisfied, you can return them and be free of the bargain," he promised, but the girl had no doubt that with the wonderful leather shoes on her feet she would be the best dancer for miles around.

And so it was. For a year the girl danced in the leather shoes, night and day, wherever she heard a fiddle play, springing high and fast with her feet never tiring.

But like her dancing heels, the year flew swiftly past. Soon the time came to fulfil her part of the bargain. However, the girl had no intention of dancing away with Old Nick. When he appeared, she greeted him with a scowl.

"These shoes you gave me were no good," she snapped. "There was no spring in them at all!"

"Really?" said Old Nick. "Haven't you been dancing in them all year?"

"Well, they look beautiful," said the girl, "but they're heavy and slow and horrid to dance in. My birch bark shoes are better."

Old Nick frowned. "You may not have been satisfied with my shoes but dance in them you did," he said. "So now you must dance away with me."

The girl put her hands on her hips defiantly. "If you don't believe my birch bark shoes are better I'll prove it," she said. "Wear the leather shoes yourself and we'll have a race to the other end of the lake and back. You'll soon see which pair are the best."

Old Nick was amused by her boldness. Certain that his leather shoes would prove stronger than her thin bark birch pair, he agreed to the race.

The girl hurried home to fetch her old shoes. When she got there she told her twin sister about the race. The two girls were so alike that they were often mistaken for each other, but the sister lived quietly at home, so Old Nick had never noticed her. To trick Old Nick, the girl asked her sister to go to the other end of the lake and wait there. Then she hurried back and gave him the leather shoes.

They took up their starting positions on opposite sides of the long, narrow lake and then off they went. As soon as Old Nick was out of sight, the girl stopped running and returned to the start but Old Nick raced along, leaping past fields and villages with great strides.

When he reached the far end of the lake he was surprised to see the girl already there. He turned at once and raced back again but to his astonishment she'd arrived before him.

"So, do you agree that my birch bark shoes are faster than yours?" she said.

"This time, perhaps," answered Old Nick, "but once is not enough to prove it. Let's race again."

The girl agreed and off they went.

The soles of Old Nick's leather shoes were now worn thin, however he was sure that the birch bark shoes must be in a far worse state. He ran and ran as fast as the wind, scattering chickens and tangling washing as he rushed past farms and villages. But, as before, the girl was ahead of him at both ends of the lake.

"She's a fast runner, all right," thought Old Nick as he caught his breath.

"Will you admit that my shoes are the best?" the girl cried across the water, but Old Nick shook his head. Sure that her birch bark shoes must now be worn to shreds, he suggested they have one last race.

This time he ran faster than the wind, flattening fences and spinning weathervanes as he rushed along like a hurricane.

But as before, the girl was ahead of him, there and back. "See, my shoes have a better spring in them," she said, "and that's the proof!"

Old Nick groaned with exhaustion. His leather shoes were in tatters and his feet were bleeding. "All right," he gasped. "You're released from our bargain. But if you stay out dancing like you do, you'll find yourself in trouble one day and then I'll be back!"

However, the girl never danced another step again, for she knew full well it was a rare thing to get the better of Old Nick!

IN FARM AND FIELD

EUROPE
A STORY FROM ENGLAND

THE ELDER TREE WITCH

IN FARM
AND FIELD

Once there was a farmer and his family who had a small herd of cows. Their farm was a lonely, windswept place without a single tree for shelter in wild weather but the farmer kept it well and his cows produced the best milk for miles around.

However, one day, when the farmer went to milk his cows he found they had no milk to give. The following day the same thing happened again.

"Something's not right with those cows," the farmer told his wife. "There isn't a drop of milk in them. It's as if they've been milked by somebody else."

The farmer depended on the milk he could sell at market, so late that night, he went out to check on his herd.

The moon was shining brightly as he walked towards the cows. Suddenly, close by the hedge he saw the shadow of a tree. The sight of a tree where no tree should be sent a shiver down the farmer's spine, for everyone in those parts believed that a witch could turn herself into an elder tree. Quickly he rounded up his cows and drove them out of the field and down to a little meadow close to the farmhouse.

"You'll be safe here," he told them and he hurried inside.

Next morning, the farmer told his family what he'd seen.

Granny, sitting by the fire, listened with a frown. "There never was a tree on this farm," she muttered. "It's something unnatural, you can be certain of it."

At that moment, the farmer's daughter who'd been out feeding the chickens came running in, as white as cream cheese.

"Father," she gasped, "there's a big tree standing in the meadow with the cows!"

"What tree is it?" asked the farmer's wife.

"An elder tree!" the daughter replied.

"I thought as much," uttered Granny darkly. "It's a witch, for sure."

At these words the family was struck with terror. The farmer's daughter ran around the house shutting the windows and locking the doors while her father fetched his gun.

"I must go out and protect my cows," he cried.

"Bravery is not enough," said Granny, "you need a silver bullet to kill a witch!"

The farmer remembered that a silver button had come off his Sunday coat and asked his wife to find it.

"I've already stitched it back on," she told him, but she took her scissors and snipped it off again.

Meanwhile, Granny stoked up the fire with wood. Then she picked up the big iron shovel that was used for raking out ash and shoved it in among the flames.

When he had the silver button, the farmer loaded it in his gun. "Now, open the door a crack," he said to his wife and he raised his gun to take aim. However, to his dismay, the elder tree had moved and now stood right in the middle of his herd of cows.

IN FARM AND FIELD

"If I shoot from here I might kill one of the cows," he whispered. "I'll have to get closer."

The farmer's wife and his daughter watched nervously as he crossed the yard, quietly opened the meadow gate and crept along the shadow of the hedge. When he was near enough, he took aim at the elder tree and fired but his hands shook so much that he missed.

At the sound of the farmer's gun the elder tree gave a terrifying shriek. She rushed out from among the cows and leaped straight at him. The farmer dropped his gun and ran for his life. He raced through the yard with the elder tree at his heels and reached the farmhouse just as her branches snatched his hat.

His wife slammed the door shut after him but in her haste she trapped the farmer by his trouser leg.

"Never mind," he shouted, "lock the door!"

A second later the house shook as the elder tree hurled herself against it in a fury. When she couldn't get in at the door she tried to get in the windows, going from one to another, beating her branches against the glass and howling like a wild wind.

The farm dog barked and the cat hissed but nothing could drown out the rattle and roar of the elder tree witch.

"I must save my cows," cried the farmer, struggling to free himself.

"Iron and fire will see her off," cried Granny. She took the shovel of red-hot coals out of the fire and told the farmer's wife to open the back door wide.

As soon as the elder tree witch heard the door open she rushed round to the back of the house. Although her old legs wobbled, Granny stood defiantly at the threshold, gripping the heavy shovel tight.

Suddenly the elder tree witch crashed through the back garden with a blood-curdling shriek. Granny waited until she was almost at the door and then thrust the iron shovel full of hot coals at her and pushed the door shut.

At once the elder tree witch burst into blue flames. Tongues of fire leaped up her trunk and devoured her branches, spitting and crackling like a bonfire. Soon there was nothing left of her but a pile of ash on the doorstep.

With great relief, the farmer's wife released her husband and he hurried out to see whether his cows had come to any harm. To his delight they greeted him at the gate as usual, ready to give him the best milk for miles around.

IN FARM AND FIELD

ASIA
A STORY FROM INDIA

THE SNAKE

IN FARM
AND FIELD

A poisonous snake came to a village one day and made its home in a hole on the riverbank. This made the villagers very afraid so they sent for a snake charmer to capture it.

The snake charmer played his flute to entice the snake to come out of its hole. But as soon as the snake appeared, it breathed at the snake charmer and he dropped down dead.

News of the snake's deadly breath kept all the other snake charmers away until, one day, a man arrived who had no fear.

First, he asked for a large quantity of unbaked clay pots. He used some to build a wall in front of the snake's hole, then he sat behind it and played his flute.

The snake soon appeared. It breathed at the pots, making them so hot that they were baked red. When the snake charmer saw this he stopped playing and the snake returned to its hole.

The snake charmer replaced the pots with fresh ones and then began to play again. This time the snake's breath only turned them brown.

When he did it a third time, the pots didn't change colour at all. The snake charmer knew then that the snake's breath was too weak to be dangerous, so he dropped his flute, seized the snake, put it in a cooking pot and placed a lid firmly on top.

"Now I must rest," he said and he lay down in the shade.

But while the grateful villagers discussed what to do with the snake, a curious boy lifted the lid of the cooking pot. At once, the snake escaped. It slid over to where the snake charmer was resting and gave him a deadly bite on the foot. Then it slithered away and was never seen again.

EUROPE
A STORY
FROM ENGLAND

**IN FARM
AND FIELD**

THE BOGEY BEAST

Once upon a time there was an old woman who was always cheerful, even though she had very little in the world.

One day she found a big black cooking pot lying in the ditch. To her amazement it was full of gold coins. "Here's treasure fit for a queen!" she cried. "I feel grand as grand can be!"

The old woman tied the end of her shawl to the handle of the heavy pot and set off home, dragging it behind her.

Before long she needed a rest. She sat beside the pot and peeped inside. To her surprise, the gold coins had turned into a lump of silver.

"That's even better," she said to herself. "Gold coins are easy to steal but a big, heavy lump of silver won't be taken so easily." So she continued on her way.

Further down the lane, she needed to rest again. When she checked the pot she saw that the lump of silver had now turned into a lump of iron.

"What good fortune," she thought. "Everyone needs a bit of iron for mending this and that. It'll be much easier to sell than a lump of silver."

But by the time she reached her garden gate there was only a big stone inside the pot.

"Perfect!" she said. "I need a big stone to keep my gate open."

However, before her eyes, the stone jumped out of the pot and began to grow until it was as big as a horse. Out shot four kicking legs, a swishing tail and a head with flashing eyes and gnashing teeth. It reared up before the old woman, screeched wildly and then galloped away.

The old woman stared in astonishment.

"Well, how lucky am I," she said. "I saw the Bogey Beast right here at my own garden gate!" And she took the empty pot inside feeling grand as grand could be.

HOME OF
THE SPIRITS

NORTH AMERICA
AN INUIT STORY

THE SPIRIT OF THE SINGING HOUSE

HOME OF THE SPIRITS

For the people of the snowy north lands, the singing house was a very special place. There, they would gather to sing the songs of their ancestors, to feast and dance around the fire, watched over by the spirit of the singing house, which was never seen but always present.

Long ago, a woman grew curious about the spirit of the singing house and wanted to see it.

The villagers warned her not to disturb it. "If you do, you'll meet with a terrible fate," they told her. But the woman was determined.

One night, she crept through the snow to the singing house and slipped inside. All was dark and silent within.

"If there is a spirit in this house, show yourself," said the woman.

A hoarse voice whispered. "Here I am, there I am."

The woman stared at the darkness but she could see nothing.

"Where are your feet?" she asked.

"Here they are, there they are," whispered the spirit.

The woman reached out and touched a pair of ice-cold feet.

"Where are your shins?" she asked.

"Here they are, there they are," whispered the spirit.

The woman reached out and laid her hands upon two shins.

"Where are your knees?"

"Here they are, there they are," whispered the spirit.

The woman reached out her hand and touched a pair of thin, bandy legs. "Where are your hips?" she asked. "Where are your shoulders and your neck?"

Each time the spirit answered, the woman reached out in the darkness.

At last she asked, "Where is your head?"

"Here it is, there it is," whispered the spirit faintly.

Then the woman reached out her hand once more but above the neck she felt no hair or bones at all. With a cry of terror, she dropped down dead!

NORTH AMERICA
A STORY FROM ALASKA

THE GHOST LAND

The chief's son was full of sorrow because his wife had died. He couldn't sleep or think of anything else, so one morning he set off to find her.

The young man walked all day and all night, following a trail through the forest until he came to a lake. On the other side of the lake he saw many people. The young man shouted across the water. "Send a canoe to get me!"

"Someone has come from Dreamland," a voice cried. "Bring him over."

A canoe was sent across the lake to fetch the young man. When he climbed out on the other side he was overjoyed to see his wife. The people there welcomed him and offered him food, but she secretly warned him not to eat it.

"If you eat in this place you will never return home," his wife said. "This is Ghost Land, you cannot stay here. Let us leave together."

That night, when no one was watching, they crossed the lake together. Then the young man and his wife followed the trail, walking through the forest all day and all night, until they came to the chief's house.

The young man asked his wife to wait outside the house while he told his father that he had brought her home. To welcome her, the Chief laid out a fine fur robe. But, to his dismay, when she entered he saw only a shadow beside his son. She hung the fur robe around her invisible shoulders and when they sat to eat, no hand could be seen lifting her spoon.

Then the young man realised that things could never be as they were before. Filled with despair, a few days later he died.

But all was not lost, for he and his wife returned to Ghost Land together and were never parted again.

HOME OF THE SPIRITS

EUROPE
A STORY FROM ENGLAND

HERNE THE HUNTER

HOME OF THE SPIRITS

Herne was the head of the king's foresters, who looked after the ancient woodland that surrounded Windsor Castle.

He knew the forest better than anyone and understood the ways of the creatures that lived there. This pleased the king, who always chose Herne to lead his men when they hunted deer in the forest.

"Herne can ride faster and shoot an arrow straighter than any of you," the king told his men. "And he knows the mind of a stag as if he were one himself!" For this, the king rewarded him with many favours.

As time went by, the other foresters grew jealous of Herne.

One night, they met secretly beneath a great oak tree in the forest to discuss what could be done to bring about his ruin. However, although they all hated Herne, none of the disgruntled foresters was actually brave enough to act against him for fear of angering the king.

Suddenly, out of the trees rode a cloaked figure on a black horse, his face hidden by a hood. The wary foresters fell silent.

"Don't be alarmed, I have come to help you," said the stranger. He told them that he lived in the woods and had heard them whispering about the head forester. "I, too, have reasons to be rid of Herne the hunter," he said. "If you leave everything to me, I promise he will soon be gone."

The foresters discussed his offer amongst themselves and decided that it suited them well. "Here's a chance to get what we want without putting ourselves in danger," they agreed, so they accepted the stranger's help.

"There will be a payment," the hooded man told them. "You must grant me one request when the deed is done. Agree to that and I shall fulfil my promise."

The foresters felt uneasy about making a promise to a stranger but reluctantly they agreed.

Then the mysterious rider took up his reins and rode away into the night.

The following day, the king and his men gathered for the hunt. As usual, Herne was given the finest horse to ride. However, when the hunting party set off he couldn't control it. Instead of leading from the front, he lagged behind, struggling with the reins as if he had never ridden in his life. When Herne finally caught up with the rest, his horse kicked the king's mount, which reared up and almost threw the king to the ground, much to his displeasure.

Herne didn't notice the other foresters watching with delight.

HOME OF
THE SPIRITS

The next day's hunt was even worse. Once again Herne found himself unable to control his horse and when he was called to display his skill at archery, which the king so often boasted about, his arrow badly missed the deer and hit a tree. The king was furious. He accused Herne of making a fool of him in front of his men and dismissed the head forester from his service.

Herne the hunter was angry and confused. He fled into the forest, tormented by the sudden loss of his skill as a rider and an archer. He knew that nobody would give him work if he had lost the favour of the king, and was filled with despair.

That night there was a dreadful storm over the forest. Deafening thunder echoed through the grounds of Windsor Castle and forked lightning split ancient trees like firewood.

In the morning, Herne the hunter was found dead at the foot of the great oak tree.

The other foresters had their wish: they were rid of Herne, but his death made them uneasy. What payment would the sinister stranger ask for in return, they wondered?

To their relief, the stranger made no appearance and they soon forgot their worries. But before long, rumours started to spread that a ghostly hunter wearing the antlers of a great stag on his head had been seen in the forest at night, chasing deer.

Sure enough, the king's deer began to disappear. The foresters knew they would be in trouble if they couldn't catch the poacher, but although they searched day and night, they found no sign of anyone.

Fear began to grow in their hearts at the thought of the ghostly rider, so one night they arranged to meet in the forest at the great oak tree to discuss what to do.

As soon as everyone had gathered there was a flash of fire and the dark hooded stranger appeared. The foresters' blood ran cold.

"I kept my promise," the stranger told them. "Now you must agree to my request. When Herne the Hunter appears you must obey his orders, just as you used to do. If any one of you fails, he shall serve me instead!" Then with a roar of laughter the stranger disappeared.

HOME OF THE SPIRITS

The terrified foresters looked at each other in alarm but before anyone could speak a familiar figure came riding out of the trees. Herne the hunter appeared upon a magnificent steed, wearing the antlers of a great stag upon his head, his face ghostly pale in the moonlight. He ordered the foresters to meet him in the same place the following night with the king's hounds, ready for the hunt, and then he rode away.

The foresters knew they had to obey. The next night, Herne led them in a wild hunt, riding without rest until dawn and killing several of the king's deer.

In the morning, although they were desperate for sleep, they had to hunt again with the king and his men.

Night after night, Herne ordered them to do the same.

The king soon noticed that his foresters were exhausted and his deer were disappearing fast. He summoned the foresters to find out why, and they were so weak and tired that they confessed to everything.

When the king discovered that he'd been tricked into dismissing Herne he exploded with rage. He ordered the foresters to be shot at the old oak where Herne himself had died of despair.

As the fatal arrows flew that day, wicked laughter could be heard echoing around the ancient forest of Windsor.

And some say a ghostly huntsman can still be seen riding there at night, wearing the antlers of Herne the Hunter.

ASIA
A STORY FROM CHINA

THE NIGHT ON THE BATTLEFIELD

HOME OF THE SPIRITS

A merchant was walking along a country road late one evening when he saw an old inn before him, whose lights were just being lit. He went inside and asked for food and lodgings.

The innkeeper shook his head. "There's no food for you here," he said. "We have just prepared a meal for some warriors who are travelling a great distance." But he took pity on the weary merchant and showed him a little side room where he could sleep.

A few hours later, the merchant was woken by loud, lively voices, speaking a language he didn't understand. He opened his door a crack and saw that the inn was filled with warriors eating and drinking.

Suddenly lantern lights shone outside the windows and a general arrived with many officers. The general was served a fine meal and when he had eaten, a young officer showed him to another room.

The merchant was intrigued by all he saw. As soon as everyone at the inn had gone to bed, he crept out of his room and peeped through a crack in the wall into the general's chamber.

To the merchant's horror, he saw the general take off his head and place it on the bed. Then the young officer who was attending him pulled off the general's arms and legs and laid them on the ground. At that moment the lamp in the room went out.

Gripped by terror, the merchant stumbled back to his bed and burrowed deep beneath his blankets.

In the morning, the merchant awoke to find himself lying outside on the ground. To his amazement, there was no inn in sight. He jumped to his feet and ran away as fast as his legs could carry him.

Along the road he met an old woman and told her his chilling tale.

The old woman smiled. "This place is covered with ancient battlefields," she said. "You don't want to be walking here at night, all sorts of unnatural things take place!"

THE
GRAVEYARD

EUROPE
A STORY FROM IRELAND

TEIG O'KANE AND THE CORPSE

THE GRAVEYARD

Teig O'Kane was a wild lad, full of bad habits. He spent his days at the races, or at the fair, and his nights roaming from one village to another, enjoying whatever party he could find.

Teig's father was very unhappy with him. "If you don't stop wasting your time and do some honest work you shan't have a penny from me when I die," he warned Teig one evening when he was home.

But Teig wasn't ready to give up his carefree life. "I'll settle down when I'm ready," he snapped at his father, and he went out for a walk.

It was a warm, moonlit night. Teig hadn't gone far when he saw a group of men walking down the road towards him, not one of them taller than a table leg. He felt a shiver of alarm.

The little men were carrying something heavy between them. When they reached Teig they dropped their burden at his feet. With horror, Teig saw that it was a corpse.

"Isn't it lucky we met, Teig O'Kane?" said one of the men, but Teig was too terrified to speak.

"Teig O'Kane, isn't it good fortune we met?" said the man again but still Teig couldn't answer.

"For the third time, Teig O'Kane," said the man, "isn't it lucky we met?" Teig's throat was so dry that he couldn't say a word. The little men smiled and winked at each other.

"Well then, as you haven't said a word we can do with you what we like!" they chuckled. "You're living a bad life, Teig O'Kane, now you must work for us."

Teig suddenly came to his senses and decided to run, but before he could escape they tripped him up and he fell to the ground. The little men held him down and lifted the corpse onto his back, then they helped Teig to his feet. Teig struggled with all his might to shake off the corpse but its cold arms clung to his chest and its legs gripped him tight. Stuck with his gruesome companion, he saw it was no use to resist.

"What will you have me do?" he asked.

"Bury the corpse," replied the little men.

Teig looked around but there was no church to be seen. "Where shall I bury it?" he said.

"Try at the church over the hill," suggested one of the men, "beneath the flagstones in the aisle. Bury it before daybreak and we'll ask nothing else. But if you're slow, Teig O'Kane, you'll work for us forever."

Teig set off with the heavy corpse on his back, muttering angrily to himself. Over the hill, he came to an old church. Teig tried the door but it was locked.

A voice whispered in his ear. "Search for the key above the door."

"Who said that?" cried Teig, breaking into a cold sweat.

"I did," replied the corpse. Teig's blood ran cold. With shaking hands he fumbled for the key and entered the moonlit church.

"Bury me now," whispered the corpse.

A gravedigger's spade lay beside the altar. Teig prised up a couple of flagstones in the aisle and began digging, but he hadn't lifted more than a few spadesful when something moved in the hole. Teig cried out and shrank away.

A decrepit figure raised itself out of the earth. "Go, go! Be gone from this place!" it wailed. Then, with a hideous moan, it sank down, lifeless once more. Teig's hair stood on end. He dropped the spade and fled from the church.

As he sat on a tombstone to calm himself, the corpse spoke again. "Bury me," it whispered.

"Where?" gasped Teig O'Kane, still shuddering at what he'd seen. The corpse pointed a bony finger. Remembering the little men's warning not to be slow, Teig set off once more.

THE
GRAVEYARD

The corpse directed Teig along many crooked roads and winding lanes until they came to a graveyard beside a ruined church.

"Bury me," whispered the corpse. Teig stumbled towards a gate. Suddenly, a multitude of ghosts appeared: ghosts of men, women and children, all pointing and mouthing words that made no sound. Teig tried another gate but the ghosts crowded round to obstruct him.

"They won't let me in," he cried.

"Walk on," whispered the corpse and it pointed the way.

Teig trudged on, crossing fields and stiles, until he came to another church standing in the middle of a graveyard. To his relief there wasn't a ghost in sight, but as he opened the gate something invisible seized him by the arms and legs. The unseen hands shook him hard, lifted him in the air, then carried him to the nearest ditch and threw him in it.

Teig sat in the ditch, battered and bruised, fearing that he wouldn't survive the night.

"Bury me," whispered the corpse and it pointed down the road. Exhausted and bedraggled, Teig heaved himself and the dead body out of the soggy ditch and walked on.

The next graveyard they came to seemed to be nothing but a collection of big stones surrounded by a wall in a field.

"Is this the place?" asked Teig.

THE GRAVEYARD

The corpse didn't answer, so, cautiously, Teig approached. Suddenly, a fiery spark appeared and danced along the top of the wall. Teig was mesmerised. Round and round it went, faster and faster, until, with a flash, bright flames leapt up from the wall, dazzling the night sky. Teig staggered back, shielding himself from the blaze. "There's no chance of getting through that," he sighed and he sank down in the grass, wishing the night would end.

But the corpse wouldn't let him rest. "Bury me," it whispered and it squeezed Teig so tightly that, despite his sore feet, he was forced to walk on.

He came to a hilltop graveyard just as a pale glow appeared on the horizon.

"Bury me here and make haste!" urged the corpse. Teig lifted the latch of the gate, afraid of what horrors awaited him, but to his relief, nothing stirred. As he searched for a spade he found a newly dug grave with an empty coffin in it. At last, the corpse released its grip and slipped off his back into the coffin with a thud. Quickly, before the sun rose, Teig closed the lid of the coffin and filled the grave.

Then, with a weary yawn, Teig O'Kane returned home. To his father's delight, from that day Teig was no longer a wild lad with bad habits but one who worked hard and never ever went roaming at night again.

EUROPE
A STORY FROM GERMANY

THE GRAVE MOUND

THE GRAVEYARD

Late one night, a soldier was passing a churchyard when he saw a man sitting on a grave mound.

"What are you doing there?" he asked.

"I'm keeping a promise," the man answered. "The rich farmer buried in this grave was selfish and greedy all his life but one day he saw my hungry children and took pity on them. He gave them food and in return he asked that I should sit all night at his grave when he died. So here I am."

"It's an eerie place among these tombstones," said the soldier. "I'll keep you company." So they sat together.

At midnight, both the men suddenly felt a chill. Out of the darkness the Devil appeared. "Get off that grave mound," he cried. "The man lying beneath it belongs to me."

"No!" replied the soldier firmly. "We don't take orders from you!"

The Devil scowled. He offered them a bag of gold but the soldier refused. "Fill my boot with gold," the soldier said, "and then we'll get off this grave mound."

"Agreed!" said the Devil with a grin. While he went to fetch some gold, the soldier cut the sole off his boot and then placed it over a hole in the ground. When the Devil returned he tipped two bags of gold coins into the boot, but they disappeared through the hole.

"You'll need more than that!" laughed the soldier.

The Devil fetched two more bags of gold. To his annoyance they still weren't enough to fill the boot so he went to get more. Several hours later he returned with a sack of gold. However, the boot swallowed up every coin.

Then the Devil flew into a rage. He reached out to grab both the men, but at that very moment the sun came up and with the first ray of light he vanished.

So the soldier and his friend collected up all the gold; half of it they gave to the poor and the rest they kept for themselves.

ASIA & AFRICA
A STORY FROM EGYPT

THE PLACE WHERE THERE WERE NO GRAVES

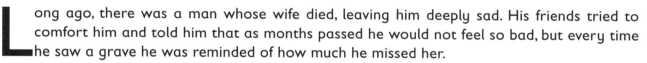

Long ago, there was a man whose wife died, leaving him deeply sad. His friends tried to comfort him and told him that as months passed he would not feel so bad, but every time he saw a grave he was reminded of how much he missed her.

"I must find a place where there are no graves," he told his friends. So he said goodbye to them and set off to find a land where nobody was buried.

The man journeyed from town to town, asking everyone he met if they knew of a place where there were no graves, but nobody could help him.

After travelling a year, along river valleys and across desert sands, he came to a town where he could see no graves at all. At last he stopped his weary search and found lodgings in the house of a sheik.

On his first night, the sheik welcomed him by serving a feast. With a great show of hospitality he offered the man some roast meat.

The man thanked him and asked politely about his family. "Where is your father?" he enquired.

"This is his leg," said the sheik, pointing to the dish of roast meat. "The rest of him is up there, on the shelf."

He explained to the man that when anyone fell ill in that town they were killed and eaten.

The horrified man didn't want to stay there a moment longer. When the meal was over, he slipped out of the sheik's house, hurried away from the place with no graves and returned happily to his own home.

THE GRAVEYARD

EUROPE
A STORY FROM ICELAND

THE GHOST AND THE MONEYBOX

THE GRAVEYARD

A young man knocked at the door of a farmhouse one day, to ask for work. The farmer there had recently died and his widow needed somebody to help in the fields, so she took him on.

Before long, the young man learned that the farm was haunted.

"The farmer's ghost has been seen walking about the fields," a neighbour told him. "He was a rich man but he kept all his money secretly buried and his wife doesn't know where, so she's been left with nothing. Now they say he returns from the dead at night to be near it."

The young man felt sorry for the poor widow and wondered if the story was true. He decided to find out.

He went into town and bought some sheets of tin and a length of white linen. First he made himself a pair of tin gloves and a tin vest, then a linen shroud to cover his body completely.

When it was dark, he stood near the farmer's grave and waited, playing with a silver coin in his hand.

At midnight, the farmer's ghost rose out of the grave. "Are you one of us?" the ghost asked.

"Yes," the young man replied and he held out his hand. The ghost felt the cold tin glove and nodded.

"Aye, you're a ghost all right," he said. Then he saw the silver coin. "That's not much to come back for!" he laughed. "If you want to see real riches come with me."

He led the young man to the edge of a field and kicked over a mound of earth. A large large moneybox was buried in a hole beneath it. The ghost pulled the box out and opened the lid. Inside were a dozen money bags full of coins.

The ghost tipped out the coins and asked the young man to help him count them. It took them a long time to count all the money; however, when they had almost finished, the young man knocked the piles of coins over with his hand, scattering them across the grass.

"Are you sure you're one of us?" asked the ghost with a suspicious look.

"Of course," replied the young man and he offered his other hand to prove it. Once more the ghost felt the cold tin glove and was satisfied. But when the coins were piled up again the young man knocked them over once more and they scattered across the grass as before. The ghost became angry.

THE
GRAVEYARD

"I swear you're alive and here to betray me!" he cried, and he grabbed the young man by the chest. To his surprise it was hard and cold.

"You see, I am just like you," the young man assured him.

With a scowl, the ghost collected up his coins again, packed them into the moneybox and buried it back in the earth. "So, where is your grave?" he asked.

"On the other side of the church," the young man replied.

"Then you go in first," said the ghost, still eyeing him with suspicion.

"No, you go first," insisted the young man.

The ghost wouldn't give way, so they argued back and forth until, eventually, dawn broke and the ghost had to jump into his grave. Then the young man immediately dug up the moneybox and took it back to the farm. There, he hid it in a barrel of water to hide the smell of earth and went about his work.

That night, the ghost was furious to discover that his moneybox had been stolen. He went to the farmhouse and sniffed around for the smell of fresh earth, but he couldn't detect anything. From his bed the young man heard a blood-curdling cry and knew his trick had worked.

Next day, the young man gave the farmer's money to his widow. A year later they were married and lived happily ever after.

NORTH AMERICA
A STORY FROM BERMUDA

COUNTING OUT THE BODIES

THE GRAVEYARD

Two fishermen who'd had a good day's catch were carrying their fish home in a basket when it began to rain.

"Let's shelter under a tree in the graveyard," suggested one of them. "We can divide up the fish while this storm blows over."

As they walked through the gate to the graveyard a couple of fish slid out of the basket. "Don't worry," said one man to the other, "we'll pick them up on the way out."

The two fishermen found a tombstone beneath a tree where they sat and started counting out the fish.

"One for me, one for you, one for me, one for you…"

Meanwhile, a boy taking a short-cut home through the graveyard heard their voices. Terrified by what they were saying, he hurried away.

When he arrived home he was pale and shaken. "God and the Devil are in the graveyard, sharing out the bodies!" he told his father.

"Don't talk nonsense," said his father.

"It's true, I heard them," the boy insisted.

"Stop making up stories," said his mother.

But the boy's sister listened, wide-eyed. "Show me," she said, so the two of them ran back to the graveyard and hid themselves by the gate.

The rain had stopped and the fishermen had just finished counting their fish. "That's done," said one fisherman to the other. "Now let's get those two by the gate."

When they heard this, the boy and his sister ran home faster than the wind and wouldn't even come out of their rooms for supper.

UPON THE OCEAN, UNDER THE SEA

EUROPE
A STORY FROM ICELAND

THE GIANTESS AND THE STONE BOAT

UPON THE
OCEAN,
UNDER
THE SEA

Handsome Prince Sigurd was admired throughout the land for his bravery and wisdom.

One day, his father the king called for him. "You will soon take my place and rule this land, Sigurd," he said. "But first, you should find a wife to be your companion and share your throne."

The king suggested that Sigurd visit his old friend, King Hardrada, who had a daughter whom many people praised. Wishing to please his father, Sigurd agreed.

The prince and his men sailed across the sea in their Viking ship for several days until they reached the kingdom of Hardrada. There, they were welcomed by the king and his daughter, Helga.

As Sigurd's father had hoped, the prince and the princess soon fell in love and Hardrada gave his consent for them to be married. A royal wedding took place with a joyful celebration that lasted many days.

At the end of the celebration king Hardrada approached the young couple. "I have no son," he said. "Will you remain here and share my kingdom?"

Prince Sigurd agreed to stay until his own father needed him.

Sigurd and Helga loved each other dearly and it wasn't long before they had a son of their own. They named him Kurt and their happiness seemed complete.

However, when Kurt was two years old, Sigurd received the sad message that his father had died. "It is time to return home," Sigurd told Helga, "for I am now king of my people and you are their queen."

When all was ready, Sigurd and his family set off in their ship to begin their new life. The sun shone, wind filled their sails and all was well, until the last day of their voyage, when suddenly the breeze ceased, the water stilled and they were unable to sail any further. Sigurd's men went below deck, out of the hot sun, to sleep. Sigurd himself soon felt overpowered by a strange drowsiness and followed them, leaving Helga and little Kurt alone on the deck.

As they played together, Helga noticed a curious boat on the water. The boat was unusually large and seemed to be cut out of stone. In it sat a huge hunched figure rowing steadily towards them.

Helga tried to call for Sigurd but to her alarm she found herself unable to speak or move. She could only watch in silence as the stone boat came closer and closer until eventually it was alongside the Viking ship.

The giantess who had been rowing the boat stepped onto the deck. She removed the queen's embroidered robes, leaving her in her white linen underdress. Then, before Helga's eyes, the giantess took on her own appearance and put on the robes. She seized Helga and placed her in the stone boat.

Helga watched, utterly powerless to resist, as the giantess took Kurt in her arms and replaced her as queen.

"Obey my words," she commanded the boat. "Do not stop until you reach my brother in the underworld." And with a powerful heave she sent the stone boat

floating away.

At once Kurt began to cry. The giantess carried him down to the king but although Kurt reached for his father's arms, Sigurd couldn't soothe him.

"If the child howls like a dog he must stay below deck," the giantess snapped crossly. "It's time to wake your lazy crew; there's wind in the sails so we can soon get off this wretched ship."

Sigurd was shocked to hear his wife talk in such a way. "Maybe the heat has overtired her," he thought.

With a fresh wind, the ship soon reached shore and the new king and queen were welcomed home. Kurt continued to cry, especially in the presence of the queen, so Sigurd found him a nurse who managed to calm him and soon he was his happy self again.

However, Sigurd was disturbed by the change in his queen who had once been so gentle and loving and now was bad-tempered and quarrelsome.

One day, Sigurd's cousins were playing chess in the room next to the queen's

UPON THE
OCEAN,
UNDER
THE SEA

chamber when they heard loud groaning. Puzzled by the strange sound they peeped through a slit in her door.

The queen stood in the middle of her room and yawned widely. To their amazement, she suddenly grew into a monstrous giantess. She stamped her huge foot and a hole opened in the floor. Out of it came a three-headed giant with a trough of raw meat.

"Here is your food, sister," said the giant and before their very eyes the giantess ate it all up. When the trough was empty, the three-headed giant disappeared back beneath the floor and, with a small yawn, the giantess became the queen once more.

For fear of their lives, the two cousins decided to keep what they'd seen a secret.

A few days later, Kurt and his nurse also received a visitor. One evening, a hole opened up in the nursery floor and out stepped a woman in a white linen underdress, with an iron ring around her waist. The ring was attached to a chain that disappeared in the dark hole below. Without a word, the woman took Kurt in her arms and kissed him tenderly. The nurse saw her love for the child and Kurt's happiness in her arms and wondered who she could be. After a short while, the lady gently handed Kurt to the nurse and disappeared beneath the floor. The following evening the same thing happened again. But before the lady left she paused.

"Twice this happiness was allowed, tomorrow shall be the last time," she said sorrowfully and then once more she descended into the darkness below.

The nurse decided to tell the king what had happened. Suspecting some strange power at work he came to the nursery the next evening to see for himself.

As before, the floorboards opened and out stepped the lady in white with the iron ring around her waist. At once, Sigurd

recognised his beloved wife, Helga. He seized her in his arms, drew his sword and cut the chain that tethered her. As he did so there was a deafening roar as the three-headed giant holding the other end of the chain fell into a deep chasm in the earth below.

Helga was overjoyed to be reunited with her family. She told Sigurd how the giantess had taken her place.

"She sent me to the underworld kingdom of her three-headed brother, who wanted to marry me," Helga explained. "There was no escape, so I promised to marry him if he let me see Kurt three times, hoping that you would be here to save me."

When Sigurd heard the truth about the imposter queen he summoned her before his court. There, his cousins related the grisly tale of what they had seen. Horrified, Sigurd ordered his guards to throw the giantess from the highest tower in the castle.

Reunited at last, Sigurd and Helga lived and ruled happily to the end of their days.

UPON THE
OCEAN,
UNDER
THE SEA

AUSTRALIA & OCEANIA
A STORY FROM NEW ZEALAND

THE SEA GOBLINS

King Rua had a young son called Toka whom he loved dearly.

One day, Toka went swimming with his friends, but he swam far further from shore than the rest and didn't return.

"We searched for him until dark," the boys told the king desperately, "but we're afraid that the sea goblins have taken him."

Rua was overwhelmed with grief. "If I have to search every region of the sea I shall find my son," he cried, and without another word he ran to a rock overhanging the sea and dived into the water.

King Rua had the gift of being able to breathe underwater, but darkness made it difficult to search the wild landscape of the seabed. He stumbled on through the night, calling Toka's name, until morning light shimmered through the water and he found himself on a sandy plain.

In the middle of the plain stood a huge wooden house. Rua guessed that it must be the house of the goblins. For a moment he marvelled at the beautiful building but as he gazed at the carving on its walls he cried out in horror – there stood his son, Toka, turned into a wooden deccoration, standing above the door.

Suddenly Rua heard a voice. "Who dares to visit the goblins' house?" asked an old woman sitting at the door.

"I am Rua, the king," he replied. "I've been searching for my lost son but the goblins have turned him to wood. Where are they? Let me have my revenge!"

The old woman's face brightened. "At last," she said, "I've waited so long for these wicked creatures to be destroyed. I am also from your world. The goblins killed my husband but they kept me here as their prisoner to be their doorkeeper. I wept when I saw the fate of your beautiful son but I had no power to save him."

"Tell me how to destroy them," said Rua.

The old woman told him that the goblins always spent their days in dark ocean caves.

UPON THE OCEAN, UNDER THE SEA

"Sunlight will kill them," she explained. "But when night falls they return home to eat and sleep. It's my duty to wake them at dawn so that they can leave before sunlight enters the house."

Rua listened thoughtfully. The old woman told him that she'd spent many hours thinking of a plan to outwit her cruel masters. "If we work together we could be rid of the goblins forever," she said. The king agreed to help.

First she told him to climb onto the roof of the house and fill all the gaps so that no light could pass through. Then he hid and they waited for the goblins to come home.

At sunset, the goblins returned. Rua listened as the spiteful creatures quarrelled while they ate. Eventually they settled to sleep and all was quiet.

"Now, block the door and the windows," whispered the old woman and Rua silently did as she asked.

When the goblins woke up the house was dark, so, thinking it was still night, they slept on.

Rua and the old woman waited until the midday sun blazed overhead, then they flung open the door and tore the covers from the windows.

At once the goblins awoke, shrieking with terror. In a panic they swarmed out of the house into the bright daylight, where they fell dead upon the sand.

The moment the goblins were dead, the spell they had cast on Toka was broken. He climbed down from the wall of the goblins' house into his joyful father's arms.

Then King Rua, Toka and the old lady returned home to their people.

UPON THE
OCEAN,
UNDER
THE SEA

EUROPE
A STORY FROM SWEDEN

THE SEA NYMPH

One summer, three fishermen spent the night in a cabin by the sea. Before they were asleep the door slowly opened and a damp, white hand reached inside. Guessing it was the hand of a sea nymph, they pretended to be sleeping.

Next day, they were joined by a young friend who had recently married. When he heard the story of the mysterious hand he laughed.

"Weren't any of you brave enough to grasp a beautiful woman's hand?" he scoffed. "If I'd been there I wouldn't have been such a coward!"

That night, the same thing happened again. The boastful young man got out of bed and clasped the white hand. Silently, he was drawn outside and the door closed behind him.

His friends waited for his return but the young man didn't appear. Next day they searched for him but could find no trace.

After three years without any sign of him, the young man's wife assumed he was dead. Eventually she agreed to marry another man.

During her wedding celebrations a stranger entered the house. A hush descended as the guests recognised the bride's lost husband.

"Where have you been?" she asked him.

"I was taken by a sea nymph to live beneath the sea, where I forgot everything," he told her. "The sound of your wedding bells brought back my memory. She agreed to let me see you as long as I didn't enter the house, but you looked so beautiful in your bridal crown that I couldn't resist stepping inside."

Suddenly the sky grew black as night. The sea nymph sent a mighty tempest to tear off the roof of the house and a deluge of rain to flood it and drown everyone inside.

A fierce torrent of water swept the young man away from his bride and when the storm subsided, he was nowhere to be found.

UPON THE OCEAN, UNDER THE SEA

EUROPE
A STORY FROM GERMANY

THE SPECTRE SHIP

UPON THE
OCEAN,
UNDER
THE SEA

Long ago, there was a young man whose father died, leaving him very little money, so he decided to seek his fortune in foreign lands.

He set sail on a ship bound for India with his father's old servant, who insisted on accompanying him.

They had been at sea for several weeks when their ship was wrecked in a ferocious storm. With no land in sight, all they could do was cling to the broken mast in the middle of the ocean and hope to be rescued.

All seemed lost until they spotted another ship on the horizon and, to their relief, the current swept them towards it. As soon as they came near, the young man shouted for help but his desperate pleas were met with an eerie silence. However, a rope hung down the side of the mysterious ship and so the two men slipped into the water and swam towards it.

When they climbed aboard, they were met with a sight that made their blood run cold: the ship's crew lay dead with their weapons in their hands and the lifeless captain was pinned to the mast by a sword in his side.

Both men were horrified. They went below deck to investigate more and found the remains of a banquet in the captain's cabin and chests of beautiful silk, fine pearls and precious jewels.

"Well, as there is nobody alive on this ship, I shall take its treasure for my own," the young man said, but the old servant shook his head.

"Where will you take it?" he asked. "We are far from land and we cannot sail this ship alone." Their hopes of rescue were dashed.

Back on deck, they decided to throw the dead crew overboard. However, no matter how hard they heaved and pulled, the sailors lay fixed to the planks of the deck as if they were nailed down. Neither could the young man remove the sword from the captain's side. He realised that

some unnatural power must be at work.

When night fell, the young man's companion went to rest in the captain's cabin while he settled on deck, away from the crew, to keep watch.

Before long, his eyes grew heavy. Half asleep, he suddenly heard footsteps and urgent cries around him. A commanding voice shouted orders in a language that was strange to him and there was a loud clatter of ropes and sails unfurling. The young man tried to open his drowsy eyes but a deep sleep overcame him and he heard no more.

Next morning, the sailors lay dead on the deck as they were the day before.

"What a strange dream!" the young man thought to himself. But he soon discovered that the old servant had also heard the ship's crew in the night.

"And I saw the captain, alive as you and me, sitting down at his table to eat!" he said, pale-faced and trembling. They decided to watch together the following night to see if the ghostly apparitions appeared again.

UPON THE OCEAN, UNDER THE SEA

At dusk, they hid in a room next to the captain's cabin and left the door ajar to watch. Once more, they heard the crew come to life on the deck above. Heavy footsteps approached and the captain entered his cabin, with the sword still in his side. He sat down at his banquet and began to eat. A while later, a sailor arrived and spoke urgently in a foreign tongue. The captain grew agitated, jumped to his feet and hurried out of the room. Angry shouting came from the deck followed by blood-curdling cries and the clash of swords and a great commotion began. After a while all fell silent.

When the two companions ventured out of their hiding place they found every man dead as before.

So it went on, night after night.

After a week had passed, the young man noticed from watching the stars that the ship was sailing towards land during the day but at night it was sailing back to where it started.

"If we roll up the sails at night and only sail during the day then we should eventually reach

land," he told his companion. So they did just that and the next morning the young man was pleased to find that the sails were still rolled up and they had not journeyed backwards. At last they could finally make some progress.

A few days later they reached land and dropped anchor.

The two men rowed to shore. At the nearest town they searched for somebody to help them remove the bodies from the ship so they could sail away with its treasure.

They were directed to the house of a wise old man called Muley who listened to their story and promised to help.

"I believe there is a curse upon those men," Muley said. "It will only be lifted by bringing their bodies to land." Muley sent for some carpenters who rowed out to the ship and sawed up the deck so that they could remove the bodies. One by one, they brought them back to shore and the moment the sailors were laid on the earth they turned to dust.

But the young man didn't want to saw off the mast to remove the captain because he wouldn't be able to sail the ship without it. So Muley brought a pot of earth onto the ship, muttered some magic words over it and tipped a little onto the captain's head.

Immediately, the captain opened his eyes and drew a deep breath. Then the young man was able to pull the sword from his side and the captain fell into his arms.

UPON THE
OCEAN,
UNDER
THE SEA

"Thank you for freeing me from my long torment," the captain sighed. "For fifty years my spirit has been condemned to sail back and forth across the sea, acting out the same terrible events. Now I have touched the earth again I can rest in peace."

"What caused this curse upon you?" asked the young man.

"I was once an honest merchant," said the captain, "but greed turned me to piracy. One day I took a holy man on board who wished to travel for nothing. Every day he lectured me about the wickedness of my life until I could bear his words no longer and struck him in anger. The blow was fatal, but before he died, he cursed me and my crew and condemned us never to live or die until we laid our heads upon the earth.

At once my crew turned against me. They killed me and pinned my body to the mast. Then they fought amongst themselves until the curse was fulfilled and every one of them was dead.

Since that day, we have neither lived nor died because we could never reach land. But now you have set us free." With that, the captain's eyes closed and, like his men, he turned to dust.

When the ship had been repaired, the young man and the old servant hired themselves a new crew and returned home with their cargo of treasure. But the strange story of their riches was a secret they kept to themselves forever.

EUROPE
A STORY FROM SCOTLAND

THE SEAL WIFE

UPON THE
OCEAN,
UNDER
THE SEA

A farmer was walking along the shore one night when he saw a group of young women dancing in the silvery moonlight. Nearby lay several seal-skins, scattered upon the sand. As he crept closer the dancers took fright. They swiftly stepped into their seal forms and plunged into the sea.

But one young woman remained, for her seal-skin lay at the farmer's feet and she was too afraid to reach for it. At once he grabbed it and carried it away to his house.

When the farmer returned, the young woman pleaded with him to give her seal-skin back. "Without it I can't return to my people," she cried. But the farmer was captivated by her graceful beauty and asked her to marry him.

As she was unable to reach her own world beneath the waves, the young woman reluctantly agreed.

The farmer and his wife lived together for many years and had several children. In that time his love for her grew strong but although she was a good wife she never seemed happy.

Often she sat longingly by the sea, where a large seal would appear and lay beside her.

Then one day, one of the children found the hidden seal-skin in the barn. When their mother saw it she gasped with joy. She kissed her children tenderly and ran down to the shore.

The farmer saw his wife clutching the seal-skin and ran after her but, to his dismay, he was too late. She slipped it on and dived into the waves and in an instant the large seal who had been her companion appeared at her side.

"Farewell!" she called to the farmer. "I loved you when I lived on the land but I always loved my first husband better!"

FROZEN
LANDS

NORTH AMERICA
A STORY FROM ALASKA

THE RED SKELETON

FROZEN
LANDS

In a small village in Alaska there lived an orphan boy. His loving father had died a few years before and with no one left to speak up for him, the villagers constantly treated him badly and ordered him about.

One snowy night, the boy was told to go out of the men's lodge to see if the weather was getting worse.

"It's cold and I don't have skin boots," he protested but the men chased him out.

The boy returned with chattering teeth. "The snow has stopped," he told them, "but it's colder than ever."

To torment him, the men sent him out again and again. When the boy returned the third time, he was trembling. "There's a ball of fire coming over the hill!" he said.

"Go out again," the men jeered, "maybe there's a whale coming over the hill!"

The boy had to obey but he soon hurried back. "The red fire is close to the house!" he cried in alarm. The men just shook their heads and laughed. They didn't notice the

boy hide himself in a dark corner.

Suddenly, a fiery figure passed across the cover of the roof hole. Everyone fell silent. Moments later, they heard a scraping sound at the entrance to the lodge and a red skeleton came crawling through the passage, creeping on its knees and elbows.

The skeleton pointed a bony finger at the village men, which made them drop to their hands and knees in the same manner. Then it turned and crawled out of the lodge and the men were forced to follow.

The skeleton led the men through the snow, towards the hill. One by one, without their fur coats and skin boots, they died of the cold.

Next morning, the village women found their men lying frozen on the ground. The boy came out of his hiding place and told them what had happened. Together, they followed the skeleton's trail until it stopped at a grave on a hillside. It was the grave of the boy's father.

NORTH AMERICA
A MI'KMAQ STORY FROM CANADA

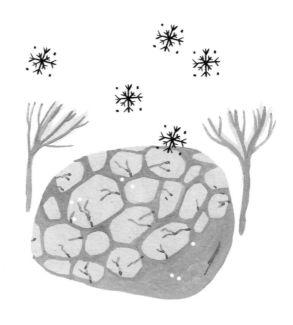

THE ICE KING

Once, there was a bitterly cold winter which lasted so long that the people of a small village used up all their firewood trying to keep warm. Several men set out to fetch more wood from the forest but none of them survived the ice and snow. One by one, the villagers died of hunger and cold until only the strongest were left.

When spring finally arrived the snow melted and frozen streams thawed, sending cakes of ice floating into the river nearby.

One man who'd survived the winter found a great raft of ice wedged into the bank of the river, trapped in a shady place where the sun couldn't melt it. The sight of the ice reminded him of the family he had lost to the harsh winter and filled him with grief.

He cut himself a wooden pole and tried to push it free.

"Be off!" he cried angrily. "You're keeping winter here. I hate you!" But no matter how hard he tried he couldn't budge it.

So the man ran and fetched his hatchet. He stepped down onto the ice and began chopping at it. Splinters of ice flew into his face. "Still trying to hurt me!" he cried. "Well, I'm not afraid of you. I hate you!"

He chopped away for hours until at last the ice began to shift. Quickly, he clambered onto the bank and seized the pole. With one tremendous heave he pushed the raft of ice into the river. Suddenly, in a spray of frost, a sparkling white figure wearing a crown of ice appeared upon it.

FROZEN LANDS

"Thank you for releasing me," said the Ice King. "Now I can go where I belong. But beware, the one you hate will return next winter!" With that he rode away upon his raft of ice down the river.

The man knew he must prepare for his enemy's return.

That autumn, he built himself a wigwam and thickly covered it with birch bark. He collected a big supply of firewood, dried plenty of meat, melted fat to make oil and made himself some warm fur clothes. Then he waited for winter.

When he woke one morning to a glistening white frost he knew that the Ice King was coming. When the air grew bitterly cold and the streams froze he knew the Ice King was near. When thick ice spread across the river itself he knew the Ice King was close.

All the while the man kept a warm fire burning in his wigwam and waited. Then one day the Ice King arrived.

The Ice King waited until the man stepped out of his wigwam and ambushed him with frozen darts. However, the man's fur clothes protected him.

Next day, the Ice King froze the man's store of dried meat but it was easily thawed by the fire.

The following day, the Ice King boldly entered the wigwam and sat down. The man was chilled to the bone by the Ice King's frozen presence, but he was unafraid. He reached for a bowl of oil and threw a handful onto the fire, making it burn fiercely. The Ice King glistened and edged away.

Another handful of oil made the bright flames leap higher. The Ice King began to melt and edged back against the wall of the wigwam.

Revived by the warmth, the man fed the fire with wood until it roared and crackled.

In the sweltering heat, water streamed from the Ice King's body. He felt his strength ebb away with every moment but he couldn't pass the fire to reach the door.

At last, he hung his head. "You have beaten me fairly," he gasped. "Let me go and I shan't come here again."

Then the man was satisfied. He raked the fire to the side and let the Ice King walk away, taking winter with him.

After that, the man never needed his fur clothes again, for it was always summer with him.

FROZEN
LANDS

NORTH AMERICA
A STORY FROM CANADA

THE GUEST

On the edge of a small village there lived a wicked old woman who used witchcraft to harm whoever she could.

One day, a stranger came to stay with her neighbour. The old woman watched them go hunting together and return with a large quantity of game.

"That stranger brings my neighbour good luck," she thought jealously. So she decided to get rid of him.

She cooked up a poisonous soup of wolf's brains, then she called one of the village boys to deliver a message.

"Tell my neighbour's guest that I invite him to supper," she said.

"What's for supper?" asked the boy.

"A soup of poisonous wolf's brains," snapped the witch, "but make sure you don't tell anyone what I've cooked."

The boy ran off and found the stranger. "The old witch next door invites you to supper," he told him. "And I mustn't say that she's cooked you a soup of poisonous wolf's brains."

The stranger thought for a moment, then he replied. "Tell her I will come."

When the stranger arrived, the old woman greeted him with a smile. But while she was busy fetching the soup, he placed a bowl under the table, between his feet.

As he ate, the stranger kept his hand in front of his mouth so the old woman couldn't see him pour each spoonful into the bowl below. When he'd finished he thanked her.

"It's the custom of my tribe for a visitor to bring a gift," he said, "so I have brought some food for you." Then he picked up the bowl of soup from between his feet and put it before her on the table.

The old woman fetched a spoon, wondering why her poison hadn't worked. But the moment her own soup touched her lips she dropped down dead.

FROZEN LANDS

108

IN CASTLE HALL

EUROPE
A STORY FROM SPAIN

ESTEBAN AND THE GHOST

Esteban travelled on a donkey from one village to another, mending pots and pans.

One day, he came to a village beside a castle. Esteban set out his tools in the square and before long people brought him things to mend. While he worked, Esteban asked the villagers about the castle.

"The castle is haunted by a ghost that wails from the chimney every night," they told him. "Many people have tried to banish it but they've all been found sitting by the fireplace, frightened to death in the morning."

"Well, I'm not afraid of a ghost," said Esteban boldly. "I shall keep it company tonight."

The villagers admired his bravery.

"I'll need some supplies," Esteban said. "Bring me lots of firewood, a frying pan, plenty of bacon and eggs and a flask of wine and I shall get rid of your ghost for you."

Eager to be rid of the ghost, the villagers

IN CASTLE HALL

brought everything Esteban asked for. When his work was done, he loaded his provisions onto his donkey and rode up to the castle.

Inside, the castle was dark and cold. Esteban carried his supplies into the great hall and put them beside the enormous fireplace, then he lit a blazing fire at one side of it and put some bacon in the frying pan to cook.

"This is the way to banish cold and fear," he said to himself.

He had just poured a glass of wine when a mournful voice cried out from the chimney.

"Oh, my!" it wailed loudly. "Oh, my!"

"That's not a very cheerful greeting," said Esteban, "but then I'm used to the sound of my donkey." And he carried on cooking his bacon.

"Oh, my!" wailed the voice again. "Oh, my!"

Esteban took no notice. He lifted the crispy bacon out of the pan and put some eggs in.

Then the voice cried, "Look out below, I'm falling!"

As Esteban lifted the eggs onto his plate a leg fell down the chimney wearing half a pair of brown trousers. He put it to one side and ate his bacon and eggs. When he'd finished the voice cried out again.

"Look out below, I'm falling!" it shouted and the other leg tumbled out of the chimney.

Esteban put it with the first leg and then tossed another log onto the fire.

Again the voice cried out and a body in a blue shirt fell out of the chimney, followed by one arm and then another.

All the while, Esteban continued cooking more bacon and eggs, which he ate with plenty of wine. "Now there is only the head to come," he thought to himself.

Sure enough, as Esteban ate his last mouthful the voice cried out once more and a head with thick black hair and a long black beard dropped out of the chimney and rolled across the floor. It joined up with the rest of its body and stood before Esteban with an anxious look in its eyes.

"Good evening," said Esteban.

"Good evening indeed," said the ghost. "You are the first person to stay alive long enough for me to put my body together again."

"That's because I brought food and firewood," Esteban explained.

Then the ghost told Esteban to follow him into the courtyard and dig a hole. To Esteban's amazement he found three bags of gold.

"I was once a thief," the ghost told Esteban. "But if you promise to give two bags of this stolen gold to the poor and keep one for yourself, my wickedness will be forgiven and I can rest in peace."

Esteban nodded solemnly. "I promise," he said and with that the ghost's clothes dropped to the ground and he vanished.

IN CASTLE
HALL

EUROPE
A STORY FROM ENGLAND

SIR GAWAIN AND THE GREEN KNIGHT

O n New Year's Day, King Arthur and his knights gathered for a feast in the great hall of Camelot castle. Before the meal began, the king asked to hear a story. As if in answer, the doors of the great hall opened and a huge green knight entered on a magnificent green horse. In his hand was a large axe.

Silence fell upon the crowd as everyone stared in astonishment. King Arthur invited the stranger to join their celebration but the Green Knight refused.

"I have come to test the bravery of your knights," he announced. "Who will take a vow to strike me with this axe and allow me to return the blow in a year and a day?"

To King Arthur's dismay none of his knights stepped forward so, to defend the honour of his court, the king himself accepted the Green Knight's challenge.

The Green Knight dismounted and offered his axe to the king. But Sir Gawain, the youngest knight of all, saw that the king was about to risk his life and he spoke out. "Let me prove my honour by accepting the challenge," he said.

King Arthur thanked him. "Strike well, Gawain," he urged, "or else you must take a blow yourself."

Then the Green Knight knelt and Gawain raised the mighty axe. With one blow he chopped off the Green Knight's head. However, to everyone's horror, the Green Knight wasn't slain; he merely picked up his head and mounted his horse.

IN CASTLE HALL

"Remember your promise," he told Gawain. "In a year and a day you will find me at the Green Chapel." And with that he rode out of the hall, carrying his head under his arm.

The year that followed passed too quickly for Gawain. When Christmas came once more he put on his armour and, with a heavy heart, rode out from Camelot to search for the Green Knight.

Gawain journeyed through the wilderness for several days until he saw a white castle surrounded by a misty moat. Tired and hungry, he rode up to the gate and was welcomed inside.

When Gawain had eaten and rested, he was presented to the Lord of the Castle. Gawain told him of his quest to find the Green Chapel.

"The Green Chapel is nearby," said his host. "But you still have three days until New Year's Day. Stay at the castle and we shall pass the time with a game."

Gawain was grateful to have a pleasant distraction from the dreadful fate that awaited him and so he agreed.

Next morning, Gawain's host explained the game.

"While I am out hunting today my wife will keep you company at the castle," he told Gawain. "When I return this evening, we shall exchange whatever we have won during the day."

The game seemed simple enough so Gawain promised to do as his host asked.

Later that day, when Gawain was alone with the Lady of the Castle she told him that she admired him and asked for a kiss. Gawain was taken aback and refused but she persisted, so he let her kiss him on the cheek.

That evening, the Lord of the Castle returned and gave Gawain a deer he had won during the day. In exchange, Gawain gave him the kiss he'd been given on the cheek.

"How did you win that?" asked his host, looking surprised.

"I promised to give you what I won, but not to tell you how," answered Gawain.

Next day, the Lord of the Castle went hunting again. When his wife was alone with Gawain she asked him to kiss her twice. As before, Gawain would only let her kiss his cheek and when his host returned that evening with a boar and a goose, Gawain gave him two kisses in exchange.

The following day, the lady asked Gawain for three kisses and offered him a love token of a green silk belt.

"I cannot accept such a gift from you, my lady," said Gawain but she insisted.

"This belt has the magical power to keep the wearer safe from harm," she told him.

IN CASTLE HALL

Gawain thought of the great axe that was soon to fall upon his neck. Although he was determined to honour his promise to the Green Knight, he couldn't resist the belt that might save him from harm and so he tied it around his waist and hid it from view.

That evening, the Lord of the Castle brought home nothing but a mangy fox. Gawain took it in exchange for three kisses but he said nothing about the green silk belt.

Gawain lay awake that night tormented by terror at the challenge ahead of him. On the morning of New Year's Day, he bid his hosts farewell and set off with a guide who showed him where to find the Green Chapel.

The Green Chapel was a cave in the hillside, fringed with green moss and ferns. Leaving his horse tethered to a tree, Gawain stepped inside and there, waiting for him was the Green Knight with his great axe in his hand.

"You have done well to keep your word," said the Green Knight.

Gawain knelt down, trying to conceal his fear. But as he saw the axe raised above his head he flinched.

The Green Knight paused. "Where is the famous bravery of King Arthur's knights?" he said mockingly. Gawain promised not to flinch again.

The second time Gawain remained still but the Green Knight stopped the axe above his head. "Now I see you do indeed have courage," he said.

Then Gawain grew angry. "Keep your side of the bargain and strike the blow!" he cried.

Once more the axe was raised but when it fell upon Gawain's neck it stopped short and only grazed his skin.

Saved from death, Gawain leapt up and reached for his sword but to his surprise the Green Knight had vanished and the Lord of the Castle stood before him, leaning on the axe with a broad smile.

Gawain realised that some magic had been at work. "So, you were the Green Knight all along!" he exclaimed.

The Lord of the Castle laughed heartily. "I asked my wife to test your honour," he said. "I spared you three times for the kisses you truthfully exchanged but the graze on your neck is for the silk belt that you hid from me. Still, you have proved yourself brave and honourable enough, young knight, your debt is paid."

Happy to be alive, Gawain returned to Camelot to tell his story. From that day on, all the knights of King Arthur wore green silk belts to remind them of their vow of honour.

IN CASTLE
HALL

EUROPE
A STORY FROM GERMANY

RUMPELSTILTSKIN

There once was a boastful girl who claimed that she could spin straw into gold. The king heard about this and demanded that she spin a room full of straw into gold for him at the palace.

The girl sat among the straw, realising how foolish she'd been. Suddenly, a little man appeared.

"What will you give me to spin this straw?" he asked.

She offered him her necklace and to her delight he accepted. He sat at the spinning wheel and spun all the straw to gold.

Next morning, the king was amazed. So he took the girl to a larger room filled with straw and asked her to transform it to gold as before.

Once again, the little man appeared. This time the girl gave him her ring and by morning the straw was spun into gold.

But the greedy king wanted more. He had an enormous room filled with straw. "Spin this to gold and you can return home," he promised.

However, when the little man appeared again the girl had nothing more to give him.

"Then promise me your first child," he said. Afraid of displeasing the king the girl agreed.

By morning the room sparkled with gold, so the king let her return home.

The girl soon forgot all about the little man until she married and had a child. Then he appeared one day and asked her to keep her promise. The girl refused.

"I'll give you three days to guess my name," the little man said. "If you succeed you can keep the child. If you fail, I shall take what's mine."

The first day, the girl tried many names but each guess was wrong.

The second day was just the same.

Then her husband remembered a song he'd heard someone sing in the wood.

"Nobody can guess my game, Rumpelstiltskin is my name!"

So next day she tried Rumpelstiltskin.

Hearing his own name, the little man screamed in anger. He stamped his foot so hard that the ground cracked open and swallowed him up.

IN CASTLE HALL

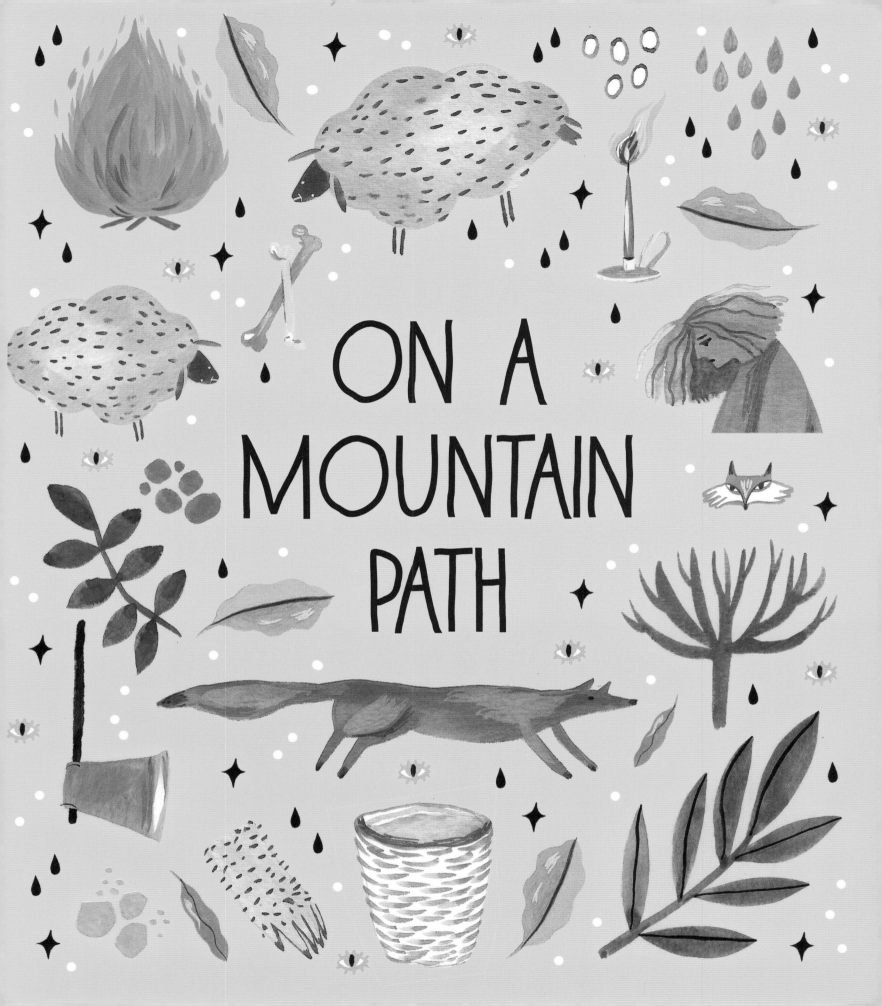

ON A MOUNTAIN PATH

ASIA
A STORY FROM CHINA

THE OLD OGRE

In the mountains of Tibet there lived an old man-eating ogre who was feared by everyone.

One day, a girl was at home alone when the ogre knocked on her door. "My mother told me not to open the door," the girl said loudly.

"But I am your mother," pretended the ogre.

The girl was uncertain. "Show me your hand through the hole in the door," she said, "so that I can be sure." When she saw the hand was hairy she knew it wasn't her mother. "You are a stranger! Go away," she cried.

"Lend me a lantern and I'll leave," said the ogre. The girl put a lantern outside the back door, hoping the stranger would go away.

But the ogre used the fire from the lantern to burn the hair off his hand. Once again he knocked on the door and pretended to be her mother. This time, she was tricked by his smooth hand and opened the door.

At the sight of the ogre, the girl ran and hid high among the roof beams. The ogre soon smelled her out but he couldn't reach her.

"How did you climb up there?" he asked.

"I piled needles upon needles," the girl replied. The ogre piled needles upon needles but he couldn't climb them.

"Tell me the truth or I'll break your bones," he roared.

"I piled cups upon cups," she said. So he piled cups upon cups but he couldn't climb them.

"Tell me the truth or I'll eat you alive," he roared.

The girl was so afraid that she told him the truth. "I piled barrels upon barrels," she said. So the ogre piled barrels upon barrels and climbed up. He seized the girl and carried her back to his cave in the mountains.

When the girl's mother returned and discovered that the ogre had stolen her

ON A MOUNTAIN PATH

118

daughter she packed some food and went in search of her.

Along the road she met a hungry fox. The woman gave him some food and in return he promised to help find her daughter.

A while later she met a hungry wolf. She gave him some food and in return he also promised to help.

They searched the mountains until they found the ogre's cave. In front of it was a pen full of sheep. The woman asked the wolf to frighten the sheep and the noise brought the old ogre running out of his cave. He threw a rock at the wolf and it fell down, pretending to be dead.

"I'll eat him later," thought the ogre. Then he saw the fox skulking around the entrance to his cave. "You'll go down in one mouthful!" he roared and he chased after it. The swift fox led the ogre away into the forest.

While they were gone, the wolf and the woman entered the cave where they found the girl tied up in a sack. Quickly they set her free and then hurried away.

Eventually the ogre grew tired of chasing the fox and returned to the cave. When he saw the sack was empty he realised that he'd been tricked. In a fury, he set off to get his revenge.

By the edge of a cliff he found the fox weaving a basket.

"You cheated me!" roared the ogre. "Now I'm going to eat you."

But the fox didn't stir. "One thousand foxes live in these mountains," he said. "I'm not the one you are looking for. I'm the basket-weaving fox."

"Well, if that's true then show me how to make a basket," said the ogre suspiciously. So the fox asked him to sit in the half-finished basket and he wove it around the ogre until he was trapped inside. Then he rolled the basket over the edge of the cliff and that was the end of the old ogre.

ON A MOUNTAIN PATH

ASIA
A STORY FROM PERSIA

AMIN AND THE GHOUL

A min was a clever boy who never liked to be outwitted. One day he was walking along a mountain path when a ghoul appeared before him. Amin saw there was no way to escape from the giant ghoul but he had nothing to defend himself with except an egg and a lump of salt in his pocket.

"I'm not going to let this ghoul make a meal of me," thought Amin, so he decided to challenge him first. Before the ghoul was close enough to notice, Amin slipped the egg into one hand and the lump of salt into the other.

"Halt, friend," he cried boldly. "I challenge you to a contest of strength."

The ghoul stopped and stared at Amin in surprise. He'd never met anyone who didn't try to run away from him. "You don't look very strong to me," he said.

"Don't be fooled by what you see," replied Amin. "I'll prove that I have great strength." He picked up a stone and offered it to the ghoul. "Can you squeeze water from this?" he asked.

The ghoul grabbed the stone and squeezed it with all his might, first in one hand then the other. "Huh," he grunted. "Impossible!"

"This ghoul is more stupid than I guessed," thought Amin, taking the stone. He put it into the hand with the egg and squeezed gently. To the ghoul's amazement liquid appeared to drip from the stone.

"That's nothing," boasted Amin, picking up another stone. "This one has salt inside. Just crumble it in your hand."

The ghoul tried to crumble the stone in his giant fist but once again he failed. Then Amin took it in his hand with the lump of salt and crushed it gently. The ghoul stared in disbelief as white grains fell through Amin's fingers.

ON A MOUNTAIN PATH

"You have proved your great strength," he said. "I need help from somebody strong like you. Come and work for me and I'll feed you."

Amin didn't trust the ghoul but he couldn't resist an adventure. "I won't be in any danger," he thought, "it's easy to outwit this fool." And so he agreed.

He followed the ghoul to his home in an enormous cave.

"I'm going to get firewood to cook the dinner," the ghoul told Amin. "You fetch water from the stream." He threw Amin a huge water-bag made from the hides of six oxen, picked up a great axe and went off to the forest.

"I can't even lift that water-bag," thought Amin but he didn't want to appear weak so he made a plan.

When the ghoul returned with the firewood, he was annoyed to find Amin gone and the water-bag lying empty, so he carried the bag down to the stream where he found Amin digging a ditch.

"Ah, there you are," said Amin with a smile. "It's really a waste of effort carrying water from the stream yourself, so I'm digging a ditch to bring water straight to your cave."

The ghoul nodded approvingly. "Good idea," he said. "You can finish that tomorrow. Now it's time to eat." And he filled the water-bag himself, heaved it over his shoulder and carried it back to the cave.

That evening, the ghoul cooked an enormous meal. Amin's plate was piled high with more food than he usually ate in a week but he didn't want the ghoul to think that he couldn't match his appetite. Luckily the cave was so dark and gloomy that the ghoul didn't notice Amin hide most of his dinner behind a rock.

Then the ghoul showed Amin a place to sleep and wished him goodnight.

However, Amin still didn't trust his host. When the ghoul was asleep, Amin put a pillow in his sleeping place and hid at the back of the cave.

Sure enough, in the middle of the night the ghoul woke up, crept over to Amin's bed with a huge wooden club and beat it seven times. Satisfied that his guest was reduced to a pulp, he went back to sleep.

When the ghoul awoke next morning he was horrified to see Amin alive. "What a bad sleep I

ON A MOUNTAIN PATH

had," Amin murmured with a yawn. "I was disturbed by an annoying insect that flapped its wings seven times."

"This boy must be a mighty demon if he felt my heavy club was as harmless as an insect's wing," thought the ghoul fearfully. Afraid of Amin's great power, he fled from the cave and ran away down the path.

Amin chuckled to himself and set off home. But he hadn't gone far when he met the ghoul returning with a fox at his heels. Amin was alarmed by the ghoul's angry expression. He guessed at once that the fox must have heard about his trick and revealed the truth.

Thinking quickly, Amin threw a stone to frighten the fox away and shook his fist after him.

"That fox deserves to be punished," Amin said sternly. "I commanded him to bring me seven ghouls to be my slaves but he only brought me you, who are my slave already!"

At these words, the foolish ghoul truly believed that a mighty demon stood before him. Terrified of being his slave, the ghoul leapt away over the rocks, deep into the mountains, and was never seen again.

ON A
MOUNTAIN
PATH

SOUTH AMERICA
A STORY FROM CHILE

THE GIRL WHO TURNED TO STONE

I n a village beside the mountains lived a local chief with his daughter Maria. Maria's mother had died when she was a child but one day her father married a new wife, hoping she would be a good stepmother.

However, the new wife had an envious heart. She was jealous of her stepdaughter's beauty and when the chief arranged a marriage between his daughter and the son of another chief, she secretly vowed to destroy Maria's happiness.

The stepmother visited a sorceress. "I need something to make my stepdaughter ugly, so that nobody will want to marry her," she said.

The sorceress gave her a jar of thick, white cream. "This is powerful magic," she warned. "It turns flesh to stone."

The stepmother smiled wickedly and thanked her.

The night before Maria's wedding, the stepmother crept into her room and smeared the magic cream all over her face.

Next morning, neighbours and friends came to see how beautiful the bride looked on her wedding day but when Maria stepped out of her room they all gasped in horror. Her face had turned to a mask of stone.

"What's wrong?" asked Maria suddenly afraid. Her father was too shocked to speak but then he noticed that one of his wife's fingers had also turned to stone.

"What have you done?" he cried angrily, staring at her hand. The stepmother looked down at her finger and realised she couldn't hide her guilt so she confessed.

Maria's father chased his wicked wife from the house and then called off the wedding.

"I shall go to the sorceress myself," he said as he comforted his stone-faced daughter. "There must be a way to undo this terrible enchantment."

ON A MOUNTAIN PATH

But when he found the sorceress, she told the chief that there was no remedy. "The cream was made from the bones of a dead man," she said. "To cure your daughter all the scattered bones need to be found."

When Maria heard there was no cure, her heart was broken. "I shall go away and live in the forest," she told her father. "I'll be happier alone, for everyone here is frightened to look at me."

So, although she was sad to leave her father, Maria went to live in the forest where she wandered far and free. There, the birds and animals weren't afraid of her stone face and became her friends.

One morning, Maria saved an ant from drowning in a stream. To her surprise, the grateful ant spoke. "Dig, dig, dig!" it said, so she dug in the earth and found some bones.

"There must be a reason that the ant wanted me to find these bones," thought Maria and so she kept them.

A few days later, she saved a toad from being swallowed by a snake. "Dig, dig, dig!" cried the toad and once more Maria found some bones.

The next day she removed an arrow from a wounded deer. "Dig, dig, dig!" cried the deer and when she did, there were more bones. Together they made a skeleton but the skull was missing.

One morning beside a mountain path she found a puma with a thorn in its paw. Conquering her fear, Maria gently removed the thorn. The grateful puma brought water for her to drink, carried in a skull between its jaws.

Maria laid out the bones she'd collected with the skull the puma had given her. In an instant a young man sprang to life before her eyes, released from a wicked enchantment. He kissed her stone cheek in gratitude and at once her own beauty was restored.

There, together in the forest, the two young people fell in love. And there they chose to remain, living happily with the puma as their friend.

ON A
MOUNTAIN
PATH

124

SOURCES

Hansel and Gretel
The Blue Fairy Book by Andrew Lang. Pub. Longmans, Green and Co. 1889

Grandfather's Eyes
Czechoslovak Fairy Tales by Parker Fillmore. Pub. The Quinn and Boden Co. 1919

Vasilissa the Beautiful
Russian Fairy Tales by WRS Ralston MA. Pub. Smith, Elder and Co. 1887

The Treasure Thief
Egyptian Myth and Legend by Donald A. Mackenzie. Pub. The Gresham Publishing Company. Pub. 1920

Little Red Riding Hood
The Blue Fairy Book by Andrew Lang. Pub. Longmans, Green and Co. 1889

The Story of the Yara
The Brown Fairy Book by Andrew Lang. Pub. Longmans, Green and Co. 1904

The Cold Lady
Green Willow and other Japanese Tales by J. Grace. Pub. Macmillan and Co. 1910

The Bunyip
The Brown Fairy Book by Andrew Lang. Pub. Longmans, Green and Co. 1904

The Snake Prince
The Olive Fairy Book by Andrew Lang. Pub. Longmans, Green and Co. 1907

Morag and the Water Horse
Scottish Folk-Tales and Legends by Barbara Ker Wilson. Pub. Oxford University Press 1954

Tam Lin
More English Fairy Tales by Joseph Jacobs. Pub. Putnam 1894

The Dance of Death
Canadian Wonder Tales by Cyrus MacMillan. Pub. John Lane, The Bodley Head 1920

The Lady of the Lake
The Welsh Fairy Book by W. Jenkyn Thomas. Pub. F.A. Stokes 1908

The Water Witch
Popular Legends of Brittany by E. Sonvestre. Pub. 1853

The Maiden in the Pagoda
The Chinese Fairy Book by Dr R. Wilhelm. Pub. Frederick A. Stokes Company 1921

The Talking Skull - Traditional

The Enchanted Apple Tree
Christmas Tales of Flanders Translated by M.C.O. Morris. Pub. Heinemann 1917

The Blacksmith and the Demon
Russian Fairy-Tales by WRS Ralston MA. Pub. Smith, Elder and Co. 1887

The Girl and the Chenoo
The Algonquin Legends of New England by Charles G. Leland. Pub. 1884

The Horned Women
Fairy and Folk Tales of the Irish Peasantry Edited by W.B. Yeats. Pub. 1888

The Blind Man and the Demons
Folk Tales from Korea by Jeong Inseop. Pub. Routledge and Kegan Paul Ltd. 1952

The Clever Goldsmith
The Caravan of Dreams by Idries Shah. Pub. The Octagon Press 1968

Yallery Brown
More English Fairy Tales by Joseph Jacobs. Pub. Putnam 1894

Old Nick and the Girl
Fairy Tales from the Swedish by Baron G. Djurklou. Pub. William Heinemann 1901

The Elder Tree Witch
Sampler of British Folk Tales by Katharine M. Briggs. Pub. Routledge and Kegan Paul 1970

The Snake
Indian Fairy Tales by M. Thornhill. Pub. Hatchards 1889

The Bogey Beast
English Fairy Tales by Flora Annie Steel. Pub. Macmillan and Co. Ltd. 1927

The Spirit of the Singing House
A Treasury of Eskimo Tales by Clara K. Bayliss. Pub. Thomas Y. Crowell Co. 1922

The Ghost Land
Myths and Legends of Alaska by K Berry Judson. Pub. A. C. McClurg and Co. 1911

Herne the Hunter
Everyman's Book of English Folk Tales by Sybil Mayhall. Pub. Dent 1981

The Night on the Battlefield
The Chinese Fairy Book by Dr R. Wilhelm. Pub. Frederick A. Stokes Company 1921

Teig O'Kane and the Corpse
Fairy and Folk Tales of the Irish Peasantry by W. B. Yeats Pub. Walter Scott Publishing Co. 1888

The Grave Mound
Children's and Household Tales by the Brothers Grimm. Pub. 1812

The Place Where There Were No Graves
Cairene and Upper Egyptian Folk-Lore by A. H. Sayce. Pub. The Folk-Lore Society 1920

The Ghost and the Moneybox
Icelandic Folk and Fairy Tales by M and H Hallmundsson. Pub. Iceland Review 1987

Counting out the Bodies
Bermuda Folk Lore by Elsie Clews Parsons. Pub. The Journal of American Folklore 1925

The Giantess and the Stone Boat
Icelandic Folk Tales by A. W. Hall. Pub. Frederick Warne and Co 1897

The Sea Goblins
Maoriland Fairytales by Edith Howes. Pub. Ward, Lock & Co 1913

The Sea Nymph
Swedish Fairytales by Herman Hofberg. Pub. Belford-Clarke Co. 1890

The Spectre Ship
Tales of the Caravan, Inn and Palace by Wilhelm Hauff. Pub. Jansen, McClurg & Co. 1882

The Seal Wife
Scottish Fairy and Folk Tales by Sir George Douglas Bart. Pub. A. L. Burt Co. 1900

The Red Skeleton
A Treasury of Eskimo Tales by Clara K. Bayliss. Pub. Thomas Y. Crowell Co. 1922

The Ice King
Indian Legends by M. F. Washburne. Pub. Rand McNally & Co. 1915

The Guest
A Treasury of Eskimo Tales by Clara K. Bayliss. Pub. Thomas Y. Crowell Co. 1922

Esteban and the Ghost
Three Golden Oranges by R. S. Boggs and M. G. Davis. Pub. Longmans, Green & Co. 1936

Sir Gawain and the Green Knight - Traditional

Rumpelstiltskin
Children's and Household Tales by the Brothers Grimm. Pub. 1812

The Old Ogre
Folk Tales of Tibet by Norbu Chopel. Pub. Library of Tibetan Works and Archives 1984

Amin and the Ghoul
World Tales by Idries Shah. Pub. Harcourt Brace Jovanovich, Inc. 1979

The Girl who Turned to Stone
Folk Tales from Chile by Brenda Hughes. Pub. George C. Harrap & Co. 1962

Brimming with creative inspiration, how-to projects, and useful
information to enrich your everyday life, Quarto Knows is a favourite
destination for those pursuing their interests and passions. Visit our
site and dig deeper with our books into your area of interest:
Quarto Creates, Quarto Cooks, Quarto Homes, Quarto Lives,
Quarto Drives, Quarto Explores, Quarto Gifts, or Quarto Kids.

First Published in 2019 by Frances Lincoln Children's Books,
an imprint of The Quarto Group.
The Old Brewery, 6 Blundell Street, London N7 9BH, United Kingdom.
T (0)20 7700 6700 F (0)20 7700 8066 www.QuartoKnows.com

A catalogue record for this book is available from the British Library.

ISBN 978-0-7112-4147-3

The illustrations were created in gouache
Set in Gill Sans

Published by Katie Cotton
Designed by Karissa Santos
Edited by Claire Grace
Production by Nicolas Zeifman

Manufactured in Guangzhou, China EB072020

3 5 7 9 8 6 4